THE LAST REFUGE

CODY'S WAR BOOK FIVE

STEPHEN MERTZ

WOLFPACK
PUBLISHING
— EST 2013 —

WOLFPACK
PUBLISHING
— EST 2013 —

Paperback Edition

Copyright © 2019 Stephen Mertz

Published in the United States by Wolfpack Publishing, Las Vegas

Wolfpack Publishing
6032 Wheat Penny Avenue
Las Vegas, NV 89122

wolfpackpublishing.com

Paperback ISBN 978-1-64119-890-5
eBook ISBN 978-1-64119-889-9

Library of Congress Control Number: 2019955506

THE LAST REFUGE

"Patriotism is the last refuge of a scoundrel." –Samuel Johnson

CHAPTER 1

*Tuesday, July 2n*d

The stars in the New Mexico night glittered like diamonds spread across black velvet. A quarter moon rode low in the eastern sky. Pale moonlight that lined the open countryside in silver did not penetrate the gnarly, intertwined branches of scrubby mesquite trees flanking a dry wash.

A four-wheel-drive SUV used only its parking lights to find its way across the rocky wash, rejoining a narrow, deeply rutted game trail that led a short distance to an unmarked van.

Bobby brought the SUV to a stop. He was a tall man. Well-muscled. Dark hair shaved military close on the sides but unruly on top. He killed the lights and engine.

Dietz, Murphy and he exited the vehicle, the three men practically indiscernible in the moonlight. They wore commando black from head to foot. Lead weapon for each man was a silenced, short, compact submachine gun. Like his men, Parnell also wore a 9mm Glock in shoulder leather. They approached the darkened van.

The night was peaceful with only the chatter of night insects breaking the stillness. A far-off coyote yipped at the moon. The leaves of the mesquite trees whispered in an errant night breeze.

One of the back doors of the van opened.

Parnell knew the ATF Officer in Charge. Chas Brown's latte features were drawn and serious in the dim light of the van's interior. Two other men sat in the van. The first was twisted around in one of the bucket seats, looking over the shoulder of the other, who manned a state-of-the-art communications console that slanted down from one side.

Brown stepped out of the van and eased the door shut, making as little sound as possible. "Hey, Bobby. It's been awhile. How's the world of covert ops?"

"Usually in another country," said Parnell.

Dietz muttered, "Ah, the heartland."

Dietz was a slim, wiry man of barely regulation height. He said, "I've fished over Elephant Butte Lake, maybe thirty miles from here. Good fishing."

The third member of Parnell's team made a rude sound. "Fishing, shit."

Murphy was a hulking African American with an old shrapnel scar that bisected his broad face from the right temple down to his left chin. Half of an unlit cigar jutted from his grimacing mouth. "Let's get this done. I've got a wife and two baby girls waiting for me at home."

Chas Brown handed Parnell a pair of infrared binoculars. "Let me show you what we've got."

He led them to the lip of a rocky ridge. They crouched to view a residential property across a county road from the top of a steep slope. A sprawling single-level stucco house with a tile roof was well removed from the nearest residence a mile away. The ridge ran several hundred yards above the southwest corner of simple barbed wire fencing that surrounded the acreage.

Parnell swept the ATN-X sight NVD goggles across the property, memorizing the layout of the main house with an attached garage, guesthouse and assorted outbuildings.

"How much do you know?" Brown asked.

"Hostage situation," said Parnell. "Daughter of a federal witness."

Brown nodded. "Courtney Milhone. Her dad was one of nine geniuses who got nailed conspiring to off a local cop and then blow up all the police and official mourners who showed up for the funeral. The kid's father rolled over and the prosecutors have the others nailed to the wall. We're talking heavy time. That is, as long as the guy testifies. That's supposed to happen tomorrow morning, but he won't say squat in court unless we can prove to him that his little girl is all right."

Murphy said, "Who's all down there?"

"The Elkins family."

Dietz growled irritably. "You need us for a family of hillbillies?"

"You've read the BG," said Brown. "Jud Elkins. Fifty years old. Former US marine with combat experience in the first Gulf War. Owns a trucking business in Tucson. He's the commanding officer of a militia based in Cochise County, south of Tucson. That's border country, porous as hell. Elkins also heads up a loosely-knit national organization of active and retired police and military personnel who call themselves the Pledge Holders. They take an oath never to take orders to disarm a US citizen or herd them into concentration camps. Their oath is to uphold the Constitution and defend us from dictatorship. Call themselves patriots. The guys on trial are in Elkins' militia and they're pledge holders. If Milhone starts naming names, Elkins is in big trouble because he was in it but behind the scenes from the funding and logistics end."

Dietz spat on the ground. "Far right nut jobs trying to kill cops."

Parnell handed over the binoculars so his men had a chance with them. "A nefarious plot to impose a one-world government on liberty-loving Americans. The enemy is the US government. Takeover by one-world agents in black helicopters."

Murphy snickered. "Take over the country, huh? Damn government can't even get Amtrak to run on time."

It was a strain of paranoia traceable back to the Civil War and even earlier, people too fearful to trust the very form of government they claimed was in danger of being lost. There was already a system in place to uphold the Constitution. It was called the Judicial Branch.

Parnell was doing his best not to show what an irritable mood he was in. He and his team were dog tired, one day out of a bloody op in Guatemala involving a CIA guy who had gotten himself into deep shit. They were en route back to Fort Bragg when central control re-routed them here. Parnell's concern tonight was that his team would not have its sharpest edge.

He said, "Chas, give us a head count."

"Okay. Jud Elkins is down there. And his wife Sandra, who stands by Jud one hundred percent. Their sons, Tod and Bo, a pair of addled war vets. Two tours of duty each in the 'Raq. And Jud's daughter. A sassy little snake they call Honeychild. She's only twenty, but don't let her tender age fool you—she's as stone cold as they come."

Dietz, a confirmed bachelor, broke into a wide grin. "Well now, it's starting to sound interesting. Honeychild, you say?"

"They're armed to the teeth," said Brown. "They think that this is a safe house, and it was until very recently but they don't know that we know they're holding the girl down there. Their guard will be up. Hair-triggered and psycho as hell."

"Any backup around?" asked Parnell.

"Standing by a half-mile from here," said Brown. "But a surgical strike is what we need to take them down and get Courtney Milhone out of harm's way. You men are the best we've got. That's why you're here."

Murphy spat out his shredded cigar. "So, let's rock. I ain't killed anybody all day."

Dietz sighed. "And we all know how testy that makes you.

Wouldn't want that."

Brown added, "If things get hot, backup won't make it in time. From here on in you're on your own."

Parnell said, "Chas, that's been the name of our game since day one. See you on the other side."

The three men in commando black moved out. The darkness below the ridge swallowed them and they were gone.

Brown stared after them and said softly enough so that only he could hear, "Good luck, you mean-ass sons of bitches."

* * * * *

They reached the bottom of the slope. A vehicle was approaching from around a curve of the blacktop road, its headlights cutting through the blackness over their heads. They froze in place behind the inky outline of squat bushes. A station wagon cruised by at the legal speed limit. Its taillights passed the entrance to the Elkins property and disappeared around another curve of the highway.

"Security?" Murphy wondered in a whisper. "No reason they wouldn't have patrols."

Dietz said, "No reason it couldn't have been folks on their way home from visiting relatives."

"Doesn't matter," said Parnell. "They didn't see us."

They crossed the road and negotiated the barbed wire fence without effort.

A pair of German shepherds came to life from the darkness near the house and charged at the interlopers, their mad barking piercing the night, their fangs bared in the moonlight.

Dietz muttered, "Bye-bye, puppies."

He muted the dogs with two silenced head shots.

Murphy winced. "That was a damn shame. German shepherds are good animals."

Dietz shrugged. "I'm a cat person."

They advanced across the moonlit property, each man covering the other two. They gained the side of the guesthouse, beyond view of the main house. Parnell issued silent orders with hand gestures. Dietz and Murphy would take the front door while Parnell gained entry from a visible rear door. They synchronized watches. Parnell held up three fingers. Thumbs up from Dietz and Murphy, who fanned out to either side and advanced on the house. They passed the closed doors of the double garage. The gravel driveway was white in the moonlight. Ten yards from the house, they broke from each other.

Moments later Parnell gained the screen door at the rear of the house. The screen door was closed; the inside door yawned open. He peered through the screen, into a darkened alcove where the square shapes of a washer and dryer stood next to a water heater. He heard inaudible conversation from somewhere in the house.

He reached his left hand out to the door handle. It was unlocked. He eased into the house. The hum of conversation emanated from the far end of a short hallway beyond the laundry room. He crouched, his index finger curved around his machine gun's trigger, his eyes on the digital readout of his wristwatch. He braced himself for the assault.

CHAPTER 2

Jud Elkins stood next to a window, inching aside its curtain with the barrel of his M-16 assault rifle. A broad-shouldered man with unruly salt-and-pepper hair and beard, his expression was fixed in a perpetual glare.

"What the hell are those dogs barking at?"

The main part of the house was an open area of high-beamed ceiling and tiled floor, equally divided into kitchen, dining and living areas. There were throw rugs and wood paneling, couches and recliners, a cold fireplace and the TV on with the sound off.

"Javelinas, most likely," said Sandra Elkins from where she was clearing the table of dishes and silverware. "They're around most every night."

She was a slim woman of medium build, in her forties. Hawk-like features. A deep cleft chin. A cigarette in her mouth wagged when she spoke, dropping ash onto the plates. A pistol was holstered at her hip.

Bo Elkins, also gripping an M-16, was at another window. "They sure stopped barking awful fast."

Bo's brother, Tod, lounged in a chair at the dining table. "Javelinas don't like dogs. Our hounds could tear one of them wild pigs a new ass except for they run in packs."

The twins were younger versions of their father in their bulky, muscular physique. They had their mother's hawk-like facial features.

Honeychild stood at the kitchen sink, washing dishes, merrily humming an off-key, barely recognizable country song. Her fatigues were a size too small, accentuating a muscular, long-legged figure.

Jud said, "One of you boys go outside and take a look around."

"I'm on it," said Bo.

Tod rose and snatched his pump shotgun from where it was propped against the table. "I got your back, bro."

Everyone wore desert camouflage fatigues except for the dark-haired girl of sixteen who was bound to a low-backed chair at the end of the dining. Her ankles were lashed to the front chair legs.

Courtney Milhone was a lanky teenager with a pierced nose ring. Her chopped hair was dyed coal black. She wore an *Unknown Pleasures* tee-shirt, black skinny-jeans and Converse sneakers that had been decorated with glitter-pen scrawled ankhs and other goth-friendly symbols. Her wrists were tied behind the chair.

Sandra Elkins said to the bound girl, "You sure you don't want something to eat, hon? I may be too hung over in the morning to make breakfast."

Courtney had grown accustomed enough to her captors for her normal rebellious attitude to resurface. "I'll tell you when I'm hungry. You're going to pay for this, all of you. You're all crazy!"

Honeychild whirled from the kitchen sink. She angrily flung aside a dishrag and grabbed a steak knife off the counter.

"That's it! I've listened to this kiddy whore's lip long enough."

The twins paused just short of the front door.

Bo chuckled. "Uh oh."

Tod said, "Wrong thing to say, Courtney."

Honeychild came at Courtney, drawing the knife back.

Sandra rushed to position herself between her daughter and Courtney.

"Jud! Make her stop!"

Jud said, "Calm down, Honeychild."

His voice was a low grumble of authority that brooked no dissent. "Put that knife down. You're stressed, that's all. Calm down."

Honeychild drew up short, staring with seething resentment at the girl tied to the chair. "But, Daddy, this bitch has been getting on my nerves! Mom was just trying to be nice."

"I told you to cool it," said Jud. "*Cool it*, dammit. Her daddy got to hear his little brat's voice one more time before he takes the stand in court tomorrow. I have explained this, haven't I?"

"Yes, Daddy. I'm sorry."

Honeychild returned, contritely, to the kitchen sink.

Sandra smirked down at Courtney Milhone. "There. See

how she listens? That's how a good girl behaves."

The front door burst inward under the force of a small, sharp explosion that tore the thick wooden door from its frame.

Murphy and Dietz flung themselves into the house, hitting the floor in dual combat rolls away from each other an instant before Jud Elkins swung about to trigger a deafening burst of rifle fire that shredded the door frame.

Courtney Milhone shrieked in surprise and fear.

Dietz came out of his roll with his machine gun spitting fire, but Jud had already dodged sideways. Bo and Tod, nearest the doorway, cut loose with their rifle and shotgun. Dietz went into a hideous death dance, the bullets piercing his lightweight body armor and pulverizing his torso, causing him to shimmy wildly under the impact of so many bullets before he toppled to the floor.

Murphy concentrated on Bo and Tod, who were tracking their weapons in his direction. He tried not to think about Dietz, poor bastard. *But you shouldn't have shot down those poor dogs.*

Parnell surged into the big room just in time to see Sandra Elkins, standing across the room on Murphy's blind side, take careful aim with her handgun and blow away the side of Murphy's head.

Honeychild stood over Courtney, her knuckles white around the handle of the steak knife.

The girl in the chair tried to draw away but could not.

Honeychild said, in a subdued voice, "Little miss have-it-all bitch. Have *this*."

The blade of the knife glinted. One swipe severed Court-ney's jugular vein. Blood geysered everywhere, across walls and people. The girl bound to the chair twitched in hideous death throes.

Parnell saw this. He heard Honeychild's laughter. He saw the bodies of Dietz and Murphy in spreading pools of blood. He swept the room with gunfire.

Honeychild gave a sharp cry and whirled, stumbling.

"Damn! I'm hit!"

Bo and Tod leapt to each take their sister by an arm. They hustled her away.

Jud and his wife opened fire on Parnell. He took a running dive behind a counter separating the stove, refrigerator and sink from the dining area. Sandra's pistol barked repeatedly, punctuating her husband's carbine firing short bursts. Par-nell hugged the floor. Bullets sent wood and plaster spraying across him. Then the gunfire ceased. The clinking of spent brass falling to the tile floor was the only sound, followed by the slam of a door. He leapt to his feet, his ears ringing despite his standard earplugs.

The big room was empty except for the dead. The door that had slammed was one of three along a hallway. The other two doors in the hallway were open. Bedrooms. He rushed the closed door. Chas Brown would have backup racing in, but these fleeting seconds here and now were all that mattered.

Parnell fired an extended machine gun burst through the door. When there was no return fire, he stood to the side of the remnants of what had been a door and kicked it off its hinges. He risked a glance inside. His bullets had gone wide, dotting a plaster wall but coming nowhere near a raised window across the bedroom.

Bo Elkins had just exited through that window. Jud and his wife already stood outside, visible in the light from the window. Jud cradled Honeychild in his arms as if his daughter was a small child. There was a splatter of blood at Honeychild's left shoulder. Tod Elkins was in the process of raising one knee over the windowsill.

Parnell said, "*Freeze!* Hold it right there."

Tod spun around to face him.

Sandra called from outside. "Come on, son! Get out of there!"

Tod tossed aside his shotgun. He laughed. There was a flush to his face and his eyes were bright. He produced a hand grenade from a thigh pocket of his fatigues. His right index finger was around the pin. "You want a piece of glory, cowboy? Come and get it."

Shit thought Parnell. He triggered his submachine gun. Nothing. The damn thing was jammed!

Honeychild screamed from her father's arms. "Tod, *no!* Daddy, don't let him do it!"

Parnell lunged. If he could get to the punk before Tod pulled the pin—

Tod laughed in his face. He pulled the pin on the hand grenade. Seeing this, Parnell pivoted to escape. But time ran out.

Reality exploded in a deafening crack of doom.

A searing white flash ended everything.

CHAPTER 3

Tuesday, August 13ᵗʰ—Six weeks later

The two things that Henri Charon hated more than anything were politics and getting up early. And here he was, up and properly attired an hour before dawn, all because of politicians living and deceased.

The windows of the master bedroom of Henri's immaculate home in the upscale Tucson suburb of Oro Valley, faced east and normally before leaving for work five days a week, he had found watching the Catalinas shifting from silhouette to deep purple crags and peaks to be a perfect way to start the day. But this morning, only his reflection stared back at him from the pre-dawn blackness of the window glass.

He took measure of the refection staring back at him. A portly figure clad in the immaculate white of a chef. Fifty-seven years old. A trace of gray at the temples, true, but not in the luxurious, fastidiously groomed mustache.

Awakened an hour earlier by the alarm clock, he had showered and breakfasted lightly on yogurt, fruit and tea while gazing at the photograph of his beloved Phoebe gazing back at him from the framed portrait's customary place, opposite him at the table. Another month and it would be the second anniversary of her death.

He had coped with this profound loss by submerging himself in his work, living for his work as before he had lived for her. He'd considered leaving Tucson, returning to Paris or New York where he would be more highly recompensed for his culinary acumen, but his love for Phoebe had first compelled him to relocate here to her beloved desert because he thought that he could not live without her. Sadly, he was finding out the hard way that he'd been wrong about that. She had loved this home and perhaps he would never be ready to leave. At least here he had the vivid memories of the best time in his life that had passed far too quickly. Leaving their home would be like losing her altogether.

The reflection in the glass blinked away such brooding thoughts. Satisfied with his appearance, Henri patted a pocket to make sure he had his wallet, and then he snatched his car keys from the dresser top and left the bedroom, walking down the short hallway that led to the carport.

It was going to be a long day.

He opened the door.

A young man, wearing black from head to foot, stood on his doorstep, pointing a pump shotgun at him. Henri was only vaguely aware of the squinting, steely eye staring down the length of the barrel at him, or of his Mercedes parked in the carport. Or of the black-clad man and woman behind the gunman. Henri felt as if under a hypnotic spell cast by the gaping muzzle of the shotgun, dark and final as death itself, aimed at a point between his eyes.

He managed to sputter questions like, "Who are you?" and, "What do you want?" as they herded him backwards into his kitchen without reply.

The kitchen was airy, well-equipped and spotless.

Bo positioned himself in an archway from which he could observe the front of the house while the pump shotgun held its bead on Henri.

Jud went to the kitchen window, over the sink, affording him a good view of a suburban residential street, caught like a painting in the glare of the halogen street lamps. Someone drove by on their way to an early job, the only visible human presence about at this hour.

Sandra carried a tote bag which she slung onto the kitchen table, knocking over the picture frame, sending the portrait face-down onto the kitchen floor with a *snick* of cracking glass.

Henri forgot about the shotgun and reflexively leaned down to retrieve the picture.

Bo said, "Leave it. Sit."

The command refocused Henri's attention on the shotgun. He sat in one of the kitchen chairs.

Sandra snapped open the clasps of the tote bag. "Strip to the waist," she instructed Henri, sounding like a nurse preparing a patient for a routine procedure.

Henri lifted a brow in indignation while never taking his attention from the muzzle of the shotgun. "But what is the meaning of this? Who are you people?"

Jud stepped across the kitchen to stand over Henri. He straightened his right arm and clasped a hand around Henri's throat. The fingers tightened like a vise, cutting off Henri's breath.

"Do as you're told," Jud pronounced each word emphatically.

Henri gasped for air, his features turning purple, his eyes popping wide with panic, soft, fleshy hands ineffectually clawing at the arm. Then Jud released his grip. Henri massaged his throat, taking in gulps of air. Jud returned to the window over the sink, dividing his attention between the deserted street outside and Henri, who reluctantly began to unbutton his shirt.

The paleness of Henri's bare protruding belly was stark in the kitchen's overhead fluorescent lights. Sandra withdrew items from her tote sack and went about affixing a small glob of silly-putty-like substance to the underside of Henri's broad stomach, using gray electrical tape to affix it, severing the lengths of tape needed from the role using her bare teeth.

Bo snickered when Henri flinched at her touch. "What's the matter, Frenchy? Ticklish?"

"But what is she doing?" Henri's French accent grew pronounced. "What madness is this?"

Jud said, "My wife is wiring you with just enough high

explosive to blow you into nothing but a stain on the ceiling and walls."

He held up a small object in his right hand. "This is a detonator. If you do not do exactly as you are instructed from here on in, Chef, well, ka-boom. No more Henri."

The purple hue of Henri's complexion paled, turned chalk white.

✳ ✳ ✳ ✳ ✳

Jud's face showed a glow of satisfaction.

They were at the top of the FBI's national Most Wanted list after the shootout in New Mexico.

Standing outside the open window, they'd been splattered with blood. That started Honeychild to screaming hysterically. For Honeychild's own good they had dropped her off at the nearest ER before speeding away into the night. Luck and survival instincts, and some *very* important friends in high and low places, had allowed them to elude capture. Most Wanted? What a laugh. Eyeglasses, dyed hair, a mustache on Jud and Bo, *and* those friends in high places...

An elderly couple had been shot down by Bo in a carjacking during their escape. Jud regretted that but Bo had gone blood crazy after witnessing his brother pull the pin on that grenade.

Sandra drew back to assess her handiwork.

"Done."

Bo chuckled. "Mom, you work fast. You're amazing."

"Thank you, son."

Jud nodded. "Yeah, good work, babe. Stand up, Frenchy."

Henri commenced regaining a semblance of his former composure.

"May I put my shirt back on, please?"

"By all means. But shake your fat ass. We've got places to go and people to see." Jud glanced from his wife to his son and said, "Phase Two."

Jud and Sandra removed their dark clothing to reveal casual street clothes worn underneath. Jud took the shotgun from Bo and held it aimed at Henri. Bo shed his commando clothes, revealing his casual street wear.

Henri buttoned his shirt, his eyes hop-scotching among them. "May I ask," he gulped loudly, "who you are?"

Sandra chuckled. "Sure you can. We're the new members of your catering crew." She glanced at Jud, indicating her holstered pistol. "We leave the guns, right, hon?"

Jud nodded, setting his sidearm on his pile of black clothes on the kitchen counter, near the shotgun that Bo set aside.

"For now, we don't need guns. We've got the cover we need. Isn't that right, Frenchy?"

Henri completed re-buttoning his shirt. He absently smoothed the shirt front with his hands. "But what is it you want of me?"

"You've got a big gig coming up today. You haven't forgotten why you're up so early?"

Henri hesitated, and then he said in a ragged whisper, "The President."

Jud said, "Here's the deal. We're leaving together now for that big gig. We're catching a ride to work with you in your Mercedes."

"Yeah," Bo said in a purring voice, "nice ride."

Sandra said, "Quiet, son."

Jud said, "We're going to show up with you at your job. We're three old friends who've been visiting and you're giving us a chance to come along and maybe catch a glimpse of the President. We'll be working as part of your catering team. There's nothing else that you have to say or do. Keep your mouth shut and get us our security ID badges at your head office while the vans are being loaded."

"That will not be easy. Getting you clearance at the last minute, I mean."

"It'll be five in the morning," said Jud. "Tail end of the night shift. A headache to deal with at the last minute. Make it happen, Henri. I've got faith in you. So, there it is. You can say no, in which case my partners here will wait outside while I blow your insides all over this nice clean kitchen of yours. Or you get us where we want to go. But if at any point you try to communicate with anyone along the way, either on your staff or with anyone else, you die."

"But...you would die because you would be close to me!"

"Don't get smart. Don't worry about us. The only thing certain is that you'll be dead."

Sandra cleared her throat. "Jud, the time."

"Yeah, right," said Jud. "So, make up your mind, Frenchy. Are you with us?" Jud raised his hand that held the detonator, his thumb on the depressor. "Or do you want to tell the world bye-bye?"

* * * * *

At the checkpoint, a Secret Service agent told Henri, "Have your people step from the vehicles. Everyone needs to have their ID ready. And we'll be going through the vehicles."

"Yes, sir," said Henri.

The catering crew stepped from the five identical white vans that were prominently decorated with the company logo, sparkling in the morning sunshine, as prim and proper as the caterers in their crisp white uniforms. Four people rode in each van.

Scrub-covered desert stretched forever in every direction. The rugged ridges of the Chiricahua Mountains rose to the north. The majestic Huachucas, carpeted with pine, dominated the western horizon. These ranges were interspersed with random foothills jutting up here and there across the high desert plain.

* * * * *

A half-mile beyond the checkpoint, a little community had been sealed off from the outside world. A small, modest church stood at a crossroads beyond the town as its last outpost, its steeple the only point visible before the mountains that reached above the rooftops. Surveillance choppers hovered about, buzzing low over the terrain. Mobile ground patrols in SUVs and ATVs crisscrossed the desert landscape.

Each caterer stood dutifully for the metal detector and a polite, thorough pat-down by sunglass-wearing, hard-faced men in black suits, overseen by grim-eyed marines who lined either side of the highway, their assault rifles held at port arms. Agents commenced a thorough search of the vans. Sparse highway traffic patiently backed up behind the trucks.

Jud, Sandra and Bo showed the forged IDs that had been previously obtained through one of Jud's militia contacts. The plastic detonation device, which needed only its state-of-the-art microchip to detonate the high explosive, went undetected in its specially designed sheath concealed by a flesh-covered patch worn just above Jud's right wrist.

It was three hours since Henri had been accosted. There had followed a twenty minute drive to the central facility of the company he worked for, where another forty minutes were spent supervising the loading of perishable and pre-pared items onto the vans while "Ted Lerner, his wife Lucy and their son Jeff" were added onto the catering staff personnel list at the last minute by the local dispatcher who, in an act considered to be of only minor illegality, waived the Lerner's security clearance requirements per Henri's assurance that they were old and dear personal friends, beyond reproach. The dispatcher knew Henri to be a man of innate honor and integrity and so believed him.

Then the two-hour drive. I-10 east out of the city. Jud, Sandra and Bo rode in the front van. Henri drove. There was next to no conversation, not even when the convoy made a pit stop at a truck stop along the way. Jud kept the radio tuned to a twangy country music station out of Benson, the town where they caught State Highway 80 south, traveling across wide-open prairie, passing through Tombstone and Bisbee, towns too small for stoplights, eventually descending the gentle sweep of the southern slope out of the modest Mule Mountains. The border town of Douglas came into view in the distance. Halfway to Douglas, they turned onto this highway leading to their destination.

Someone on the White House staff had contracted the same five-star catering firm that had previously catered three separate Presidential affairs and many lavish events for regional politicians and high-profile public personalities. But background checks could only go so deep on such short notice.

The agent who stared into Henri's eyes must have read the nervousness he saw there as the normal reaction of a civilian under Secret Service scrutiny.

Within minutes of its arrival, the convoy of white vans passed through the checkpoint.

CHAPTER 4

Marine One is the official air traffic control call sign for the Sikorsky VH-3D Sea King helicopter carrying The President of the United States. The bulky aircraft, painted in Marine Green, swept in to provide The President and First Lady with their first view of Dry Mouth, Arizona.

Dry Mouth was called Dry Mouth when first named back in the mists of time it was so far from the nearest source of water, that's what you'd be experiencing by the time you got there.

The town was appropriately named, perched at the remote crossroads of a blacktop county road and a paved state highway, only a few miles north of the American/Mexican border in the southeastern corner of Arizona. Population: 232. Median yearly income: $17,813. The estimated number of households was 106.

Dry Mouth was comprised of a main street with a couple of dozen businesses, diners and a library. There was an auto shop at the eastern end of town. Outside the town limits, dirt roads angled off from the highway, lined with homes of varying vintage on assorted sized lots, mostly one-story structures, adobe with wooden frame, and some mobile homes. A trailer park squatted adjacent to the county highway. The RV park along the state highway was closed for the season.

The Sea King gently touched down on the improvised landing pad behind the church. The pilot initiated systems shutdown.

In a cabin comfortably appointed much like a den, complete with home entertainment center and a wide variety of DVDs, CDs and oaken book-lined shelves, The President unbuckled his seatbelt. Martin Harwood, POTUS, exuded a straightforward style and grace that the public and the media had taken to. He was a vigorous man. Five-foot-ten. A solidly built one-eighty. His face was naturally round, but with strong features and striking eyes that were penetrating and direct.

The First Lady sat beside him. Ten years his junior, she was well turned out for what was sure to be a major photo op. She was a well-coifed redhead wearing a somber yet stylish summer dress of modest length, belted at the waist, matching pumps, a tasteful string of pearls, earrings and a just-short-of-glitzy hairdo.

Their four-man Secret Service detail were in position just outside the cabin in preparation for debarkation; four nondescript men of athletic build, chiseled features and the standard issue dark suits and sunglasses.

A veil of dust, kicked up by the backwash of the big chopper's rotors, began to settle beyond the two-inch-thick bullet proof tinted windows, providing a view of the scene on the ground.

Commercial shuttle service helicopters sat nearby. Limos were everywhere. The media had set up camp in an open field across from the church. Towns people stood behind the security lines, gawking for a look at the Washington VIPs who had been arriving throughout the morning. Everywhere was the highly visible Secret Service presence. Snipers were positioned on rooftops. Suited men roamed the dusty streets.

The agent at the cabin door, as if speaking to his cufflink, gave an affirmative to someone in a quiet voice and then said to The President, "They're ready outside, sir."

The morning was crisp and clear, the sky a turquoise blue with fluffy cotton ball clouds.

A beautiful day for a memorial service.

Jefferson McDaniel. Dead at 97. An American institution, they'd started calling during his final days and for once the accolades rang true. A legendary diplomat. Highly decorated Vietnam War hero. Brilliant military career and the political savvy that led to his appointment as national security advisor before serving as secretary of state. The cigar and western attire were McDaniel trademarks; always a *bolo, never* a necktie even in the halls of Congress and at the UN general assembly. Jeff McDaniel had been America's unerring compass through the shifting sands and alliances of a post-9/11 world, his consul sought by ranking policy makers well after his official retirement.

This was the largest mass gathering in recent history of the elite of the US government. All the living Presidents and their wives were gathered here today to pay their respects. Many of the pols present today had gotten their start, to varying degrees, thanks to a helping hand from the silver-maned statesman whose rich baritone was now silenced forever. Jeff McDaniel had been born and raised in Dry Mouth, Arizona and out of respect for his enormous contributions to his country over a distinguished forty year career, the policy makers, the power brokers of government, had converged on this tiny little hamlet in the middle of nowhere to honor the man in a memorial service, his ashes having been scattered from an airplane across his beloved Huachuca Mountains the day before.

The President rose and extended a hand. "Ready, hon?"

"As ready as I'll ever be," said the First Lady.

She ignored his extended hand. She rose and stepped past him.

They had not slept together in more than a year.

CHAPTER 5

Kelly Conley was just finishing a clutch job on a fifteen-year-old Chevy when a white County Sheriff SUV turned into the gravel parking lot of her small auto repair shop.

Mike Wilson was behind the wheel. He was a deputy sheriff who lived in Dry Mouth with his family. Someone sat in the front passenger seat, not in back like a prisoner would. Sunlight reflected off the windshield, concealing the passenger's features.

Mike stepped from the vehicle. He had a husky build. Square-jawed good looks. Wiry, close cropped black hair. His khakis were pressed, and his highly polished black shoes shone in the sunlight.

Like most of the locals, they had known each other all their lives.

"Morning, Kelly."

"Hey, Mike."

"Not going over to the church to see the President?"

Kelly shrugged. Her brunette shoulder-length hair was tied in a ponytail that extended from the back of a baseball cap. Her denim coveralls were relatively clean this early in the day.

"I've got a world of respect for Mister McDaniel, bless his heart, but right now the living and their car troubles are keeping me too damn busy."

She and Mike had been an item once upon a time. Years ago. High school stuff. Before Mike met the pretty Mexican-American girl in Douglas who was now his wife. They had three kids, aged six to two. In a town the size of Dry Mouth you stayed civil and moved on when a relationship ended.

Mike said, "I brought over an old friend who wants to say hello."

The passenger emerged from the far side of the SUV.

Kelly thought, *Well I'll be damned.*

Jack Cody looked almost exactly as she remembered him from seven years ago. A big guy ruggedly built. Dark hair worn too shaggy to be respectable. A backpack was slung over his shoulder. He still carried himself with that loping, panther-like grace.

The three of them stood in the shade of the old adobe building that housed her shop.

"Hi, Jack."

"Kelly."

She said, "Damn you. Why'd you run away?"

His eyes were still that same clear blue that matched the

Arizona sky on a day like today. He said, "If it's any consolation, I ran away to something a hell of a lot worse." His eyes had seen things since she'd last looked into them. Those blue eyes had become windows to a hardened, perhaps haunted soul.

Mike cleared his throat. "Kelly, don't be that way. We're old friends, right?" He elbowed Cody in the ribs. "I was glad to see him. He was walking this way."

She said, "I'm sorry, Jack. It's good to see you."

They glided effortlessly into a chaste hug between friends. She was well aware of his well-toned body in that fleeting moment. Oh, yes. There was a muscle-toned hardness to him that hadn't been there before.

The three of them—her, Mike and Cody—had once been the best of friends, which had made for a difficult summer after high school when the romantic triangle between them raged at a fevered hormonal pitch. When fall came, she was Bud's girl. Cody left town. He vanished; destination unknown. A year later Mike met the pretty Mexican girl in Douglas.

Kelly commanded her breath to remain steady. Years ago, she had stopped thinking about ever seeing Jack Cody again. She had recently ended a year-and-a-half relationship with a ranch hand from up the road who had then wandered out of the area and out of her life. She was used to cooking for one and reading herself to sleep. She owned a TV but didn't watch it much. She had come to love her solitary life, her routine, the work. She liked sleeping alone.

And here was the best lover she'd ever known.

Damned if she would ever tell him that. It pissed her off that her first concern upon seeing him again was the ten pounds she'd gained since he'd last seen her.

Mike said, with a laugh, "Everything going on in town today and our man decides to drop in."

Jack indicated the activity audible from the direction of the church. "Imagine my embarrassment when I realized all this hoopla wasn't a welcome home party for me."

"They'll all be gone by tonight," said Mike. "Then things will be back to normal. But, uh, Kelly, we do have a problem."

Kelly nodded. "The town is supposed to be sealed off to everyone except locals and the visitors from Washington."

Mike nodded. "That's why I gave him a lift here."

Jack said, "I'm a local."

"Seven years ago," said Kelly. "Where do you hang your hat these days?"

"I've sort of been wandering this great nation of ours. Seeing the sights."

She frowned. "You're a drifter?"

"A restless spirit. A seeker of wisdom. Don't worry, Kel. I was honorably discharged from service three months ago."

Something within her relaxed and melted. *Watch it,* she told herself. "And where are you passing through to, oh restless spirit?"

"I'm not sure."

"Well then, how on earth did you manage to get into our sealed-off town?"

"I can't tell you. All I can say is the guys patrolling out

there are damn good. I'm better."

"And you took this risk…why?"

He grinned and some of the haunted look left his eyes. "No risk to me. Like Mike said, I was in the area and started thinking about old friends and the old days, so I decided to drop by and make the rounds and say hello. I wasn't about to *not* come into town just because there were some people around who didn't want me to. That's not my nature. So here I am."

"And that," said Mike to Kelly, "is the problem. I figured this would be the safest place for Jack to lay low. It's just until tonight. Then it won't make any difference whether he's in town or not."

Jack was watching her for a reaction. "If it's a bad idea, that's okay too. I can just keep on walking."

"Well actually, Jack," said Mike, "no, you can't. See, the Feds have rolled over us big on this, as you can imagine. I'm supposed to pick up and turn over to the Secret Service anyone I find who doesn't live here. Sorry. Nothing personal. It's my duty."

"I know about duty," said Cody. "I respect the law and I respect you, Mike. Let's get together tonight for beers at the Bright Spot after you get off duty. The three of us."

Kelly said, "So I have nothing to fear if they find you here?"

"I'm restless," said Cody, "I'm not trouble."

"That," said Kelly, "certainly depends on one's point of view." She sighed. "Okay. I'm sure Jack and I have plenty of catching up to do."

They watched the County Sheriff Department SUV leave

the gravel parking lot and drive off down the street.

Kelly said, "Have you seen David yet?"

David was Cody's brother; his only surviving relative. David was the assistant pastor at the community church.

"Maybe I'll surprise him. But the last time we spoke he was pretty clear about us taking different paths in life and him not wanting to see me again until I'd, how did he put it, oh yeah, until I realized what was important in life."

"He never forgave you for not coming home when your mother was dying."

"I couldn't. Other people's lives depended on me. I tried to make him understand."

"He will in time," said Kelly. "I'm sure David prays on it. He's done a lot of good and touched a lot of lives in this community. Your brother's a good man."

"Never said he wasn't," said Cody. "But let's talk about you. A mechanic, eh?" He used the tip of his index finger to brush away a smidgen of engine grime from one of her cheekbones. A mischievous glint came into his eyes, touched the corners of his mouth. "I've always said that you can't get too friendly with a good mechanic."

Kelly lifted her chin, "Jack Cody, am I going to have trouble with you?"

And damn if he didn't answer with nothing but a grin.

CHAPTER 6

The caterers paused in the performance of their tasks to watch for the President and the First Lady to emerge from Air Force One. The oversized helicopter dwarfed the humble church. The church, one hundred yards from the canopied dining area, was cordoned off by practically shoulder-to-shoulder Secret Service personnel.

Another dozen plainclothes agents were stationed in and around the dining area where tables were arranged in twin rows from beneath one end of a broad, rectangular canopy to the other. Every seat provided an expansive view of the surrounding Southwestern landscape. The tables were set, silverware and napkins and water carafes in place, in readiness for the memorial luncheon that would follow the service.

Jud Elkins was readying a display of dessert pastries. Sandra and Bo were putting the finishing touches on nearby place settings.

Henri was going through the motions of preparing for the

memorial luncheon, issuing commands like a field general. Jud had instructed Henri to stay close to him, and none of the other caterers were aware of the pure terror in their leader's eyes.

The President and the First Lady walked arm-in-arm, appearing properly somber, toward the front entrance of the church, their personal four-man security unit walking apace. The twin front doors of the church had stained glass windows set in them and were held open by the pastor, a portly, white-haired man in his late fifties, and a younger assistant pastor. They wore wide, guileless smiles of greeting. The stained glass colors conveyed warmth in the morning sunlight. The red buds of ocotillo plants were festively arranged on each side of the entrance. These were the vital seconds when the President was most vulnerable, an exposed target in the open. The agents would accompany him only as far as a vestibule just inside the front entrance, beyond which point everyone was already seated in plain wooden pews, awaiting the service to commence, it having been determined that with such tight security, the sanctity of this humble little crossroads church would only be blasphemed by the presence of weapons.

A dark-suited agent, making his routine rounds, approached Henri and Jud, coming down the aisle between the rows of tables, eyeing everything and everyone, assessing every threat and angle of attack, seeking out details that didn't fit.

Jud whispered to Henri without moving his lips.

"Boss me around."

Henri blinked. "I beg your pardon?"

"Do it now, goddammit, or I'll blow you to kingdom come. Yell at me or your fat belly is all over this place."

Henri then also noticed the Secret Service man approaching. He understood.

He erupted at his people. "Layabouts! Stop gawking! You can watch yourselves on the television tonight. Right now you belong to me."

Henri gestured at Jud for emphasis. "This man knows that time is money. Observe the precision with which the pastries have been arranged. Back to work, all of you! Snap snap!"

The Secret Service man strolled by.

Jud growled, "I said yell at me, but I guess that was good enough."

Henri mopped his sweating brow. "It was the best I could think of, *monsieur.*"

"Shut up. And you're in America. Knock off the *monsieur* shit."

"As you wish." Henri returned to his duties.

An unbidden image flitted across Jud's mind, so real he could almost reach out and touch it. *His mother, taking him to a tent revival meeting when he was a kid, under a tent like this wide canopy that covered the dining area. His brothers and sisters would find chores to do and nothing could budge Pa. But as the youngest, Jud had no choice but to accompany his mother, a slim, plain Christian woman with an unshakable devotion to her faith.* So long ago, thought Jud.

Sandra and Bo angled over to join him, apart from the

activity around them.

Sandra said softly, "It's happening, Jud. Just like they said it."

"Did you think it wouldn't?"

Bo said, "Those high ups in Washington may have bank-rolled this thing, but you sure are the smart one, Daddy, putting it into action."

Jud smiled—to himself as much to his son's compliment. *And it won't be the only thing I'll action, he thought, but I gotta wait until the time is right.*

The President and the First Lady reached the front entrance of the church. Two of their security detail hustled inside ahead of them. The second pair of agents followed the couple inside.

Jud lifted his cell phone and thumbed a speed dial number.

He whispered into the phone, "Initiate."

✳ ✳ ✳ ✳ ✳

The fifteen-foot-long vestibule on the other side of the church entrance was just wide enough for the President and the First Lady to walk through side by side.

Mrs. Harwood unhooked her arm from her husband's as they moved into the cool shade. The President looked at her with a sideways glance but decided against trying to put his arm back through hers again.

Perhaps she was just observing solemn protocol, but Pavlina had the knack of making sure even that observance sent a piercing a hot needle of anger through his heart. He would deal with it later he told himself, when they got back to the White House, no point of making something of it now.

The two agents ahead of the President turned around in one smooth movement at the inner doors leading to the main body of the church.

Beyond them in the stained glass dappled interior, the President could see the coffin on trestles in the aisle before the altar. There was a huge picture of Jefferson McDaniel on an easel next to it surrounded by wreaths and tributes. In the picture McDaniel was standing with the Capitol Building behind him, his arm held high in a wave, his electric smile like a light house beam. In the photograph he was full of life, full of energy—it seemed so at odds with the huge copper handled coffin, and the stillness within the church.

The President's eyes flicked back from the coffin, momentarily distracted again by his two secret servicemen. They had not parted yet to allow the President and his wife access to go through to the Church.

The two agents behind had stopped in the vestibule, and the President could hear the chatter of background radio communications from their earpieces.

President Harwood and Pavlina stopped before the two agents who had turned.

He was used to waiting for secret service protocol to be observed when he was on official business like this. But as far as he understood it, the building had already been passed *Go Green* by security control—the ring of agents around it would make it one of the safest buildings in the United States right now. There would be helicopters at stand-off above the near-by hills ready to employ ECM if terrorists were to attempt a missile attack on it, there were jets on standby at several nearby airfields ready to intercept anything coming into the projected airspace. There were soldiers on the ground around the town of Dry Mouth making sure the routes in and out were sanitized. And yet, here they were. The two agents ahead, turned to face the President and his wife, blocking their progress, as if the final say so for them to enter for the service had not yet been given.

One of the agents behind wasn't content with the situation either. The President heard him clear his throat before he spoke. "What's the hold up?" the agent said from behind. "We're good to go. Eagle is cleared to enter."

The agents in front of the President, Pickles and Blint – both dark haired, cut from stone, wearing suits that looked like they been painted on, drew their SIG Sauer P228 9mm pistols and fired four shots between the President and the First Lady.

President Harwood pushed his wife to the wooden floor, sprawling across her. They went down hard, her knee pushing bonily into his side, pushing out a gasp of pain. There were two more shots and thuds as other bodies hit the deck, followed by the involuntary twitching of someone's heel vibrating momentarily against the floor as death finished its progress through a body.

He looked up and his gut bucked to see that Pavlina's face

was smeared with blood. Thankfully, there was no visible injury—it was not her own blood.

Screams came from the body of the church off the back of the gunfire. Pickles said to Blint. "Crowd control. Now."

The President heard footsteps pounding into the church and Blint shouting. "Anyone moves and I'll execute you where you stand! Be quiet or die!"

Harwood , breathing hard, trembling and terrified, felt Pickles' free hand reach into the back of his collar and the President grunted as he was yanked off his wife.

Pavlina was frozen. Her eyes fixed on the two dead Secret Service agents who had been behind them. Their heads had been opened up like cans popped in a fire. Brains and blood slithered from their wounds.

Harwood was on his feet now. Pickles put his SIG in the back of his neck. "You want to stay alive you do everything I say the nanosecond I say it. Understood?"

The President nodded.

"You, bitch." Pickles said to the frozen First Lady. "Get up or I give your husband a sunroof."

Pavlina blinked. Bit into her bottom lip and then began to move. First onto her knees and then up to her feet. She looked at Harwood , and then to Pickles.

"Shut the doors, bitch."

It was as much as Pavlina could do to step around the two dead agents, but still managed to leave a couple of bloody footprints as she reached out, pulled the doors closed and the Arizona brightness was curtailed.

Harwood could hear his heart in his ears. He knew there were enough agents outside in Dry Mouth to invade a small country. He'd been trained enough to know that all he had to do would be to co-operate, and that there would be security teams springing him and his wife from this, probably in a matter of minutes. He held out his hand to his wife as Pickles ground the gun into the back of his neck.

Pavlina took his hand. It shook between his fingers, and her eyes were smeared with tears. This time there was no hesitation. She wasn't going to be scoring any more points against him today.

"It's going to be okay," Harwood said to Pavlina.

"No, it isn't," hissed Pickles.

CHAPTER 7

Sara Durell's lunch break didn't go the way she wanted it to. These days just getting a lunch break was a win. But it's been well known for millennia all the best plans are made by mice and women just for the express purpose of giving God a good laugh.

It started well enough, finding herself unexpectedly between meetings when an intelligence briefing finished early. She suddenly had a whole hour to herself to fill. This led to her getting out of her blue business suit in the bathroom, changing into her sweats, and jogging out of the office onto the humid Washington afternoon.

The gym where she was member was just a block and half away. She didn't like to use the gym in the Agency's Washington Building. There were only so many times she could avoid getting hit on by agents before she hit one back with a fist. And as she hadn't managed to get any recreational exercise for a few weeks this was an opportunity she wasn't going to pass up.

The day was humid and gray, a flat lid of cloud over the city that buzzed with the heat and made dark patches of perspiration around her armpits. She cursed that she'd been in so much of a hurry to get out of the building, that she'd left her water bottle on her desk.

Sara's dry mouth made her pick up speed, the sooner she got to the gym, the better.

Up the stairs, through the glass doors, and the air conditioned cool of the gym greeted her with a pleasant welcome after the muggy street. The pale pine and glass plated reception area with its palms, and minimalist furniture was quiet and oddly deserted. True, Sara didn't get many chances to come to the gym on her near non-existent lunch breaks, but the absence of anyone in reception was a surprise.

At the back of the reception area there was a glass wall between Sara and the business end of the gym—treadmills, spinners, and cross trainers, and again, as she stood there with the sweat drying in the chill, she realized the whole area beyond the glass seemed devoid of people too. The screens above the treadmills, and the peloton bikes were on, but were only showing there was zero activity to drive the individual statistics for any member who might be operating them.

Behind the reception desk was a pine door leading to a back office. The door was open, and as Sara approached, she could hear the low murmur of voices. Someone was whispering. It was too quiet for Sara to make out, but the whisper had the edge of concern. Sara leant over the desk and tried to get a look inside the office.

Sara jumped as the glass door into the gym slammed open and three men in their sweats bounded out past her as if they were being chased by hell hounds. Without a word they stormed across the reception area and crashed through the doubles doors out onto the street taking the steps three at a time and then sprinting across the road through the traffic.

Sara reached into her pocket for her phone.

Suddenly a picture of it sitting on her desk, next to the bottle of water made her wince. She'd left that behind too. Something was going on, and the cold damp feeling in her gut told her that it was more than serious.

The doors to the gym were still open, and she could hear voices through it. Nobody in there was whispering, there were cries of shock, and other voices exclaiming surprise.

Sara remembered that dreadful September day when the world had shifted on its axis. When those two towers had come tumbling down. She had watched opened mouthed as on the TV the first tower had begun to crumble and collapse—vividly reliving the shattering sight of replay after replay of the planes slamming into the buildings.

Sara had that same feeling of dread now as she walked into the gym.

At the far end of the gym, she knew, in a cool down area that couldn't be seen from reception, there were a number of screens which would run news channels without sound.

The chyrons skimming at the bottom of the picture and the flicking graphics would only raise occasional interest in those sitting on the seats. But now as Sara moved in the gym area proper, she could see a glut of men and women in their gym gear crowding beneath the screens, looking up. Some were running their hands through their hair; others had their hands over their mouths.

It was a tableau of concern and shock.

Sara walked nearer, focusing on the picture that was duplicated on both screens even though they were set to show different networks. A church in a shimmering Arizona morning. The doors closed. The stained glass in those doors shattered by gunshots. Agents, police and civilians near a tent running for cover, Air Force One on the ground, marines taking up defensive positions around it.

And then she was close enough for the words on the chyrons ticking below the pictures to resolve themselves into horrible truth.

Sara only had to read them once before she turned and sprinted from the gym.

"Hostage Crisis. President and First Lady held by terrorists in Arizona Church."

* * * * *

As Vice President Clara Maddox Mulray's Deputy Chief of Staff, Debbie Langwith knew her job sometimes was made more difficult than it needed to be, by a boss who wasn't known for walking well behind the line of public outrage.

In many respects, Mulray was the anti-Harwood . And that was why he had picked the forty-year old West Virginian

Senator to be his running mate.

Mulray could always be relied upon to liven up the news cycle with an off color tweet, a combative interview, or an opinion piece on an outré website, that would energize Harwood base but also crucially deflect the heat from his controversial policy agenda when he needed it.

In that aspect, above all others, Harwood was the steady hand, and Mulray was the time bomb with only three ticks left.

Mulray was incredibly popular in the country but had always been seen as a maverick on the Hill. She might have turned into quite the opponent of Harwood if he hadn't brought her inside the tent to pee out, rather than stay outside it to urinate in.

In many circles it had been seen as a masterstroke of political strategizing; in other opinions it had been a mistake of monumental proportions.

Debbie didn't care which way the wind blew on Mulray's appointment. All she was concerned with was ensuring that the Vice President's mess always landed on the paper, not the carpet.

Debbie was a smart and ambitious thirty-six-year-old political operator, who had worked her way up the party ladders after her academic career in public policy research and several stints on the boards of Fortune Five Hundred tech companies.

Debbie had come highly recommended to Mulray from Harwood's office to fill the role of Deputy Chief of Staff. She worked well with Darren Hadrian, Mulray's campaign man-

ager and a likeable Texan who had become the titular Chief
through familiarity and as a thank you—so it was Debbie who
did most of the donkey work and heavy lifting with the staff
and the office.

She preferred it that way, was given a free hand to hire and
fire, and was working diligently to further bolster the team
working for the Vice President, to turn them into a force in
waiting. Harwood wouldn't be President forever, and there
would come a time when Mulray would run for the highest
office herself, and Debbie wanted to be in the best position to
point her own career in that direction.

Big picture, Debbie, big picture she'd tell herself when she
would want to put her head in her hands at Mulray's latest
off-color utterance. *You may be cleaning up trivial stuff now,
but that's going to put you in pole position later.*

Today was no exception.

Mulray had been overheard, well, recorded—by a guy
on his mobile phone—at a prayer breakfast, questioning the
parentage and mental competence of one of the most widely
respected members of the Supreme Court.

The Vice President might have got away with it if the
hissed stream of Anglo-Saxon which had accompanied her
less than complimentary assessment of his judgement hadn't
dominated the news cycle since the story had broken late last
night. Say what you like about the Bench—that was ok, but
blaspheme at a prayer breakfast? That was a much tougher
sell.

Debbie was waiting outside Mulray's office in the White

House, ready to go in and talk to her about how they were going to roll this back. She was going to recommend they should apologize without apologizing, and how they were going to spin it into a jokey piece of satire the Vice President had said off-the-cuff to a friend. They'd move the focus onto the political motivations of the guy who had recorded the conversations, get some dirt on him, counter leak it, and have the story moved off Mulray onto the wider concerns of privacy and politicians being humans too. Debbie reckoned that by five that evening they will have turned the oil tanker of the news cycle a couple of degrees away from Mulray and onto something else entirely.

Well, that was the plan.

Debbie looked at her watch. She'd been waiting fifteen minutes now outside the firmly closed doors. The secretary's desk outside the Vice President's personal office was empty. That usually meant that Cortina Lane, Mulray's prissy, fastidious but competent secretary was in the office with Mulray and Hadrian. Which probably meant they were talking campaign business, which meant they were not focusing on the day's really important prayer breakfast flub but were looking towards reelection. Mulray was an "ever-forward kinda gal" as she'd said on a bazillion occasions to Debbie when she'd tried to get the VP back onto the important stuff. "Just fix it," she'd say with a wave of her hand, and Debbie, with a sigh, would.

She looked at her watch again.

Twenty minutes now. She was due to meet the head of

ways and means in ten minutes, and she'd have meetings domino-ing into each other for the rest of the day if she didn't get her time with the VP now.

She reached out to knock on the door. Nothing ventured...

"Miz Langwith! Move aside please!"

Debbie's hand hovered over the wood as she became peripherally aware that bodies were storming through the doors behind her. A hand fell on her shoulder and she was pushed roughly out of the way as eight secret service agents burst like a tsunami of muscle past her and opened the door to Mulray's office.

The seat of a sofa had met the back of Debbie's knees, and she crashed down onto it as the agents streamed into Mulray's office.

There was a strangled cry of "What the hell..." which Debbie recognized as Mulray's voice followed by a firm, "You will come with us Madam Vice President," and then almost as soon as the wave of agents had broken, they were backwashing out of Mulray's office with the tall, blonde haired VP in the middle of the men like Fay Wray clutched in King Kong's fist.

As soon as they had come they had gone and an eerie silence descended. Debbie put her feet back on the carpet, and stood up, brushing herself down and straightening her skirt.

White haired and craggy Darren Hadrian and thin as a straight razor Cortina Lane came from Mulray's office, their faces covered in shock and concern.

"What's happened?" Darren asked Debbie.

"No idea. Was there a drill planned for today? I usually get a heads up from Colin," she replied.

Darren shook his head. "Beats me."

"OMG." said Cortina. She was looking at her smartphone. She turned the screen around to show Darren and Debbie.

Debbie was running for the door before Darren could get a word out.

CHAPTER 8

Mike had gone back into town to ensure the hoopla around the church wasn't getting out of hand.

The President being in town for McDaniel's service was the biggest thing that had happened in Dry Mouth since *Dinosaurs Roame*d *the Earth* and he should be around to show that Dry Mouth PD—which was the grand name they used for one sheriff, two deputies, and an office above the public library—could be relied upon to help out the people of town when the White House Machine was rolling all over it. "Folks around here don't take kindly to being told where they can and can't walk. I know they all loved McDaniel, but I'm pretty sure only a minority of them voted for McDaniel, so there might be certain...tensions I'll have to deal with...back there," he'd said slyly as he'd got back in the SUV before driving off, leaving Cody and Kelly in the auto shop.

"Certain tensions?" Cody had said with a wry grin.

"I do declare I'm sure I don't know what he's talking about.

Mercy!" Kelly replied in her best Southern belle. They'd laughed, and she'd left the Chevy to fix itself while she pulled them both a beer from the refrigerator at the back of the oil stained garage.

They sat, he in a near collapsing armchair, and her on an old office chair on which the leather was split, and the yellow foam beneath was making a good attempt to escape.

"You wanna talk about it, Jack?"

"What?"

"The tension. I guess you asked Mike to drive you over here."

Jack smiled. "Busted."

Kelly grinned back and took a swig from the can. She had thought about Jack a lot when he had first left town. But like all fleeting things, they fade into the background eventually and become part of the tapestry of one's life. It wasn't until Mike had brought Jack over this morning that she realized how much she had missed him. Here he was sitting at the back of her shop, smiling up from the ancient armchair, large as life and twice as beautiful.

"How long you planning on staying?"

Jack shrugged. "Depends."

"On what?" she said, taking another sip from the can.

"Tensions."

Kelly howled and dribbled beer out of her nose. "You bastard! You waited until I drank that didn't you?"

Jack winked. "Maybe."

Kelly wiped her lips and chin dry on her cuff. "So really,

how long do I have you for? Do I have to use you up all at once
or do I get a chance to ease myself back into things?"

"Honest answer, I don't know. I'm just following my feet
these days. Been…a tough few years. Still trying to work out
what's important and what…what I can let go."

"Sounds like something you need to talk over with your
brother at the community church, not something you need an
old flame for."

"Perhaps my feet led me here for both. Let's just say I'm not
planning on moving on just yet. If David will talk to me, then
I'd want to see him just because he's my brother, not because
of any wise council he might offer."

"Sounds sensible."

"Yeah. After the past few years, that will make a change
for me at least."

"Wanna talk about it?"

"Maybe after a few more beers and a bite to eat."

"Deal."

"But maybe not at all."

She smiled. "It's okay, that doesn't make it a deal breaker."

Any reply Cody might have made was suddenly drowned
out by a siren sounding, shattering the sleepy afternoon here
on the outskirts of Dry Mouth.

Jack and Kelly stood and looked out through the open end
of the auto-shop to the road outside. Two National Guard
SUVs zoomed past, fast as brush strokes, sirens blaring. Behind them a line of four, no *five* ambulances, raced by at the
heels of the SUVs. Then two troop carriers, a little slower,

with men in the open backs working at their weapons, looking along sights, checking magazines, their faces worried, eyes nervous.

"Something's going down," said Cody.

"Nah, they've been around Dry Mouth since yesterday. Driving about, putting up their roadblocks, enjoying being the big I am. You heard Mike; the townsfolk don't take kindly to being pushed around. Even for the President."

Jack shook his head and repeated. "Something's going down. I've seen guys getting ready to go into an active situation a million times. Those National Guardsmen are not on their way to man a roadblock."

"Then what could it be?"

"You got a TV in here?"

The media scrimmages around the church were being pushed back as a tighter perimeter was enforced. The reporters and crew were complaining and bellyaching, but they were assertively corralled by agents back to the vans. They were told to move back another five hundred yards, well into the town. From there they were only just able to glimpse the wooden church spire through the buildings.

Under the tent, Jud and the others, still in their chef's gear had been told to wait by other agents until they were given the order to move. Bo and Tod could hardly wipe the smiles of their faces, and Sandra had had to whisper to them a couple of times to change their expressions.

Jud knew that they only had a couple of minutes before the agents decided to sanitize the catering area and moved them back beyond where even the media were stationed. It would only take one smart mouth comment from Bo or Tod to arouse suspicion of a keen agent and they might be having their ID checked more thoroughly, and questions being asked of the Henri and the other staff.

Henri himself looked like he'd been frozen in ice. His eyes were bulging, and his lips were a tight thin line. Jud gripped his arm, and leaned into his ear, looking for all the world like he was going to say something supportive, when his intention was just the opposite. "Listen, Frenchy, you chill the hell out now, or I'll chop you up like sushi. Me and my family will be out of here in a couple of minutes and you'll be coming with us. You really don't want me to leave you here and blow you up like a firework, do you? Because I will. I really will."

Henri's face relaxed, and fluid started to leak out of his trouser cuff.

"Aww," hissed Jud, "Henri have to go pee pee?"

Color reddened Henri's cheeks, but he nodded and made an attempt to untense his shoulders.

"Good boy," said Jud, and giving the Frenchman's arm another cruel squeeze that made his eyes wince closed, he leant away to whisper to Sandra.

"Pickles is taking his time."

"We don't know how long the congregation are going to take to suppress. Pickles will come through. He knows the score."

"We're too exposed here," Jud breathed, the tension for the first time showing up in his voice. He didn't like to show weakness in front of anyone, let alone his family, but as the heat beat down out of the Arizona sky, and the desperate flitting of agents, marines and national Guardsmen continued around them he was getting antsy.

What had started as a little local difficulty had snowballed in ways he couldn't have imagined—especially when the movers and shakers had got in touch with him while they were on the run and told them what the potential for action could be.

They had offered him the Intel, the seed cash, contacts, the explosives and the weapons to carry out this audacious plot. They seemed to mesh perfectly with how Jud saw the world, how to fix its problems and the Elkins clan would be spirited out of America to live out their lives in luxury.

Obviously, Jud had had to give himself a good talking to make sure that the luxury he had been promised would be in line with his beliefs that, as the elites could not be trusted, that he wouldn't be joining their ranks. But a nice house, a sum of money and changed identities wouldn't go amiss if they got what they wanted today.

There was of course one extra thing Jud would want to achieve from the action against the President, but that could wait until the time was right, and his high-falutin' contacts wouldn't be able to object. But achieve it he would.

Sandra's elbow tapped into Jud's side. "Look. Here we go."

The door to the church opened, and a thick set man, with a halo of white wavy hair around his head came out with his hands up. In the darkness of the vestibule behind, Jud could see Pickles, still wearing his dark glasses and suit, pointing his gun at the back of the man's head.

The troops and agents ducked down behind their vehicles, and all pointed their guns towards the church.

"I'm Reverend Henry Just," and man shouted. His voice was thick with fear and cracked on his surname. "This is my church. The President and the First Lady are alive and will stay that way if everyone does as they're told."

An agent called over the hood of his car, the barrel of his gun not dropping an inch. "Send the President and the First Lady out, and then we can talk."

Jud saw Pickle's lips move and his SIG push into the back of the Reverend's neck. "Get ready," he whispered to Sandra and took Henri's wrist. If the Frenchman was going to run, now would be the time he would do it. Jud's iron grip compressed the chef's flesh around his arm bones. "Move and you'll never make a soufflé again, Frenchy."

Reverend Just put his hands even higher, "There will be no negotiations until the rest of their operatives are in the building. I will count down from three…"

More whispers from Pickles.

"And when I reach zero, all of your men will point their guns to the dirt. Failure to comply will result in the death of First Lady Pavlina Harwood."

"Now hold on…" called the agent.

"Three…"

The agent was unwavering with his gun.

"Two..."

Another agent leant into the ear of the one who had spoken. There was a harsh exchange of words.

"One..."

The agents looked at each other's faces. Both were grim and drained of color.

"Z..."

"Do as he says! All guns down now!"

The men around the church did as they were told. All guns went down. Reverend Just's knees sagged, and it seemed like Pickles almost had to hold him up.

"Excellent!" said Jud. "Let's do this."

Jud yanked Henri forward, and with Sandra and Bo in a train behind him, he led them towards the church, smiling and waving as he went.

Under the tent, Tod moved back into the shadow of the canvas.

CHAPTER 9

Jack watched the white coated caterers walk up the steps into the church on the TV screen. One of the news networks had managed to find a vantage point outside the cordon, but high enough to still see across to the church. Kelly was biting her thumb. Cody was rubbing his chin.

Something was indeed going down, and it was no surprise the National Guard and ambulances were high tailing it towards town as if their tails were on fire, because basically they were.

Jack assessed the perimeter the agents had set up as best he could, and although there was no sound being transmitted from around the church on the network, it was clear that those going up the steps were not becoming hostages, but they were in some way coordinating or were at least reinforcements. There would have been little chance of them getting into the church before whoever had taken it over because of the rings of security. That they were dressed as caterers meant they might have had a contact within the President's security team to at least get them near enough to the action to be able to be walked through when the time came.

This suggested to Cody that this was indicative of some sort of inside job. That changed the rules of the game from the kickoff. Opportunism is one thing—gunmen hiding in plain sight on the off chance they'd get a shot at the President as he walked into the church—but this was a whole magnitude of trouble higher. A hostage situation was bad enough, but one where the leader of the free world was the target, and that target had been taken was beyond remarkable.

Jack, purely as an assessment of the technical ability of the terrorists—and yes it wasn't too early to be using that term—meant he already had a grudging respect for them.

Respecting the enemy was always the first step on the road to beating them.

"I can't believe this is happening," said Kelly, hugging herself.

Jack shook his head. "If you don't plan for the unbelievable, you're more likely to be sneaked up on. I'm hoping some wise guy in the Secret Service had planned to have plain clothes agents in the congregation already. Kinda like air marshals. You might have total faith in your security, but unless you make contingencies for the unexpected, you're dead."

"Don't say that."

"Sorry, just spit-balling aloud. I need to make contact with Washington. Can I use your cell?"

She passed him the iPhone from her back pocket, eyes still fixed on the TV they were watching in the rooms above the auto shop. She lived simply, one bedroom, one kitchen, one living room, one bathroom. They'd come up the stairs at the back of the building just three minutes before, but Jack already knew as much about how she lived that he would need to. The place was clean, smelled a little of cooking from the night before, and the furniture was solid if not flashy. A bookcase held as many auto manuals as it did novels. Her reading ran the gamut from Danielle Steele to Dickens. Stopping off at Stephen King and James Patterson along the way.

"So, you don't have your own phone? Why?"

"People tend to call me." Cody thumbed a number into the screen and waited for it to ring. It was only while he was waiting for the call to get connected that he remembered where his brother worked. Inside that church. The one that would be on every TV screen pretty much in the world.

He sighed inwardly. David may no longer have a choice about not wanting to see him, there was a good chance, once he'd made this call that Cody would be seeing him one way or the other.

"Agent Durell?" Sara's voice was clipped and tense, as if she'd been in the middle of another conversation entirely.

"Hey, Sara, are you busy?"

Under the circumstances his lame attempt at a joke was way over the line. He heard her breath suck in, and her voice went up an octave.

"Jack? Where the hell have you been?"

"Around. I'm being here now. You want to hear from me or not?"

Although Sara Durell was still notionally his CIA handler, they had got closer than either of them had liked in the past, and where circumstances had pulled them apart, now they were bringing them back together.

"You've been out of contact for three months, Jack! Three months! And I guess you've seen the news and you make contact because it amuses you, doesn't it? You're a liability, Jack Cody, and I don't have time to play games with you right now."

Jack sighed. He was due the ear mangling. Yes, he'd been out of contact for three months, but when you're deciding what it is you're bothering to stay living for, that took a lot of thought, and walking those highways had given him a lot of time to think.

"I'm not playing games, Sara. There's two things you need to know right now."

"Okay I'll bite, go on."

"One, my brother David is inside that church."

"We know, and we're going to get him and everyone else out of there alive. What's the other thing?"

"I'm in Dry Mouth. Want some help?"

＊ ＊ ＊ ＊ ＊

"But I'm the Governor!"

"I don't care who you are sir. You're not going into the red zone."

The roadblock had been set up across Dry Mouth's main street. There were the regulation diners, hardware stores, shoe shops and supermarkets. There was a crowd, and there was Arizona Governor Frank Kellerman, who had already walked four hundred yards from his limousine which had been stopped way back by other National Guardsman. He'd left his driver with the limo and stomped up to the road-block—which consisted of four SUVs, nose to tail across the black top, stopping all traffic to and from the vicinity of the church.

"I'm supposed to be at the service!"

The Guardsman looked at Kellerman like he was regarding a slow kid in kindergarten. "There is no service. Not now."

"That's preposterous! I've driven here all the way from Phoenix! I demand to speak to your superior officer. I want your name. I want your service number. I want your mother's maiden name. I'm going to kick your ancestors back to the two-bit country they came from! Let me through, dammit!"

"Governor Kellerman?" Mike peeled out of the crowd and approached the two men at the roadblock. All Kellerman seemed to notice was Mike's uniform. "Ah! The law at last. Tell this lame excuse for a National Guardsman who I am and why he should let me through."

Mike nodded to the guard in an *I'll handle this* way, and so the guard took a step back—but where he was now standing would still not allow Kellerman through.

The standoff was permanent.

Mike smiled. "I'm afraid I don't have the authority to do that Governor, but if you'd like to come back with me to Dry Mouth PD, you'll be able to use that as your base of operations until we can figure out how your experience and skills can be best used to assist the people of Dry Mouth at this time."

"I know when I'm being BSed, young man."

"Believe me, sir, that's the last thing on my mind, but the situation at the church has changed. This isn't the normal security cordon. There has been an incident."

Kellerman hadn't heard about what had happened in the church. The limo had punctured a tire fifteen miles outside Dry Mouth, and Kellerman had been sleeping off a heavy night of extra-marital debauchery while his driver had fixed it—which is why the radio was off, and he'd set his smartphone to *Do Not Disturb.* The first he'd heard of what had happened to the President was when Mike, walking him over to the library and the iron steps up to Dry Mouth PD, told him.

Mike couldn't be sure that among the concerned noises Kellerman was making about the situation, he thought he'd picked up a little relief mixed in there, because the politician was glad he hadn't made it to the church on time.

The Dry Mouth PD offices were buzzing. Not because of activity from the Police Department. Sheriff Haines was in the church with the other hostages, and Dry Mouth's only other Deputy, Logan Brayne was visiting his sick father in Albuquerque. There was never much trouble in Dry Mouth, and sometimes Mike and Logan would be so bored they'd race each other to a cat up a tree just to see who would get there first.

If truth be told, he was glad that he was pretty much in charge now with his boss and his brother deputy off the scene.

So much so that he'd ingratiated himself on the local ABC News affiliate, by allowing them to set up a camera position against the window of Haines' office, for the view across the rooftops to the church.

The reporter, Brittany Franco, a neat and well turned out thirty-*mumble* woman with long black hair, full cheeks and eyes as blue as 50s diner neon, caught sight of Kellerman with Mike and pulled her cameraman around from the window.

"Governor Kellerman, do you have an update for us?"

Mike was amused to see Kellerman had clocked Brittany before she'd seen him and had already straightened his tie and smoothed back his hair.

"I'm awaiting a situation report from Dry Mouth PD, and Sheriff's deputy…" he squinted at Mike's ID badge, "Wilson here, and once I am fully apprised of the facts, and the rest of my team get here, we will of course be making a full statement."

Brittany's face darkened like a thunderhead and she motioned her cameraman to go back to the window.

"No one knows anything. We have no idea if the President is alive, we have no idea what the demands of the terrorists are, and the Governor of Arizona knows less than nothing…"

Brittany turned back to the window, saying, "…at least that last one we knew already."

Mike winced, but Kellerman was oblivious to the slight that had just been visited upon him.

His fingers were stabbing at the live feed on his phone. Something on the screen had animated him greatly. "Mike, I need you to call my office. Tell them to get my people down here right now, to this building."

Mike could just see on the small screen what Kellerman was referring to. His gut clenched and his heart began to hammer. He looked out of the window towards the church to confirm in real time what he was seeing on Kellerman's screen.

"My God." Kellerman said. "Are they insane?"

CHAPTER 10

Jud couldn't help the smile breaking out all over his face has he surveyed the inside of the church.

Pickles and Blint had done well.

McDaniel's coffin, picture and floral tributes had already been pushed to the back of the church to clear the aisle.

The mourners had then been moved from the pews to the right side of the church and knelt with their hands on top of their heads, eyes down on the floorboards.

There were around sixty of them all told, a mixture of locals, and a smattering of national figures who had made the trip to Arizona. A larger, more formal service of remembrance for McDaniel had been planned to take place weeks later in Washington—this funeral had been asked by the family to be a more private affair—that was until President Harwood had indicated that he would wish to attend.

The fact that his poll numbers were slipping a little nationally had nothing to do with it, his press secretary had assured a skeptical press corps back in Washington.

Pickles had quartered off anyone he thought might present difficulties to their mission. There was a grizzled guy in a sheriff's uniform. Name badge: Haines. He was against the opposite wall. There were two men kneeling next to him who had had their jackets removed, and Jud could see empty shoulder holsters beneath their arms. Next to them were Reverend Just and a curate, both in black, heads down, fingers interlocked through their hair.

The bodies of the two Secret Service agents who had been killed had been dragged into the church, leaving a thick smear trail of blood across the varnished floor. They had been placed side by side, as much to clear the vestibule as to show the congregation what would befall them if anyone stepped out of line.

Sandra and Bo pushed Henri to his knees next to the holster guys on the *trouble* side of the church. He was sniveling and crying, tears dripping from the end of his nose.

But the prize, as Jud walked between the wooden pews down the center aisle, had been reserved for the altar. There, covered by Blint with his SIG was the President of the United States and the First Lady. They knelt side by side, facing the entrance to the church hall and they were both watching as Jud made his way towards them.

Jud felt like a prince advancing towards his coronation as king.

Harwood began to speak, but his voice was cracked and dry. He coughed to clear his throat and tried again. "I don't know who you are..."

Jud held up his hand to silence the President. "You will, Harwood, you will."

The President plowed on. "This situation isn't going to end well, for any of us. You realize that, I hope?"

Jud shrugged. "We have contingencies in place. We have backup plans, and we have the greatest guarantee of our safety we could possibly wish for."

"And that is?" Harwood fixed Jud with a hard stare that amused him more than it worried him.

"We have you, Mister President. We have *you*."

* * * * *

Bill Haines was a year off retirement, and he was damned if he was going to end his career as Dry Mouth's sheriff on his knees while the leader of the free world was held at gunpoint by a bunch of terrorist scum.

He may not respect Harwood as a politician—too wishy washy on too many issues for Bill's liking—and he may not have voted for him, but it wasn't Harwood up there on the altar with a gun trained on him.

That was the Republic. That was the Flag. That was the *Idea* of America, and Bill wasn't going to stand by while that Idea was trashed.

While the thin faced guy in the chef's whites spouted a bunch of nonsense about how they had their *greatest guarantee* of safety, Bill surveyed the body of the church.

He was just twelve yards from the entrance. The pews were empty of people, but they were solid and would provide some protection from bullets if he kept low enough. One of the traitor agents was covering Harwood and the First Lady on the altar. The other was in a position that would give him a good arc of coverage for the main bulk of mourners on one side, and Bill's group on this side of the church.

The woman and the boy who had come in with Mr. Confident were walking away from the crying guy and pretty much had their backs to Bill. If they carried on another four or five steps, they would give the agents with the guns possible pause if Bill got up and ran, if he could keep them between him and the shooters.

It was a harebrained scheme he knew, but if only he could get to the vestibule things might change in his favor. There Bill knew, in light of the number of church, synagogue and mosque shootings in the US over the years, Reverend Just kept a snub nosed detective special in a small cubbyhole beneath the collection box.

Bill knew about it because he'd suggested it to Reverend Just in the first place. He'd helped Reverend Just pick out the gun and had taught him how to shoot it. It was only there for emergencies, but Bill knew it was there.

And this was the mother of all emergencies.

If he could push off from the wall, keep the newcomers in the line of fire just for the three seconds he figured it would take him to get to the vestibule, then he might be able to get to the gun. He might just be able to give these scum a little of their own medicine in return.

This wasn't about saving Harwood, this was about defending the Idea of America. This was what Bill had pledged to protect and serve as a sheriff.

The woman and the boy only had to take one more step and...

Bill fell forward onto his hands, and then pushed off the back wall with his feet. He was up and running.

His calculations had been correct. The traitor agents were shouting at the woman and the boy to get down.

A shot splintered the corner of a pew as he ran low by it. The wood, as Bill had hoped had saved his life.

He was five yards away as bullets began chewing up the floorboards around him. Women were screaming, the traitors were shouting. The wooden wall near Bill's hip blew apart as the agents got line of sight now the woman and the boy had dived to the floor.

Bill made it into the vestibule, as a welter of bullets exploded all around him. A searing pain in his left shoulder buffeted him to one side. He didn't have time to check if the pain was from a bullet or splinters of wood exploding as the result of gunfire, but it hurt like hell.

He swept the collection box aside, lifted the flap and almost yelped with joy as he saw the gun there in the warm dark. He reached in and gripped the gun, turning back towards the aisle as he did so.

Years of muscle memory and police ritual made Bill shout, "Police officer! Drop your weapons!" but he was already firing. The agent on the altar had already pushed the President and the First Lady onto their faces and was returning fire. Bill shot at him first as he dived out of the way. Mr. Confident was anything but, he was backing away with his hands up as Bill fixed the detective special on his chest.

The crashing impact on his back was accompanied by the clatter of a short burst of machine gunfire.

As Bill hit the ground, the cold spinning from his fingers, he realized he'd been shot from behind.

As the black boots of the SWAT team attacking the church pounded past his ears, his last thought was that he'd been shot by his own side.

CHAPTER 11

"No! No! No!" the words burst from Cody's mouth as he watched the SWAT team swarming up the stairs of the church with shields held ahead and Heckler & Koch MP5 submachine guns spitting muzzle flashes.

The TV screen froze and went black as the transmission was cut.

"What happened?" Kelly said, thumping the TV remote to try to make the picture come back on. But even as she did so the network cut back to the studio, where a flustered anchor explained that they wouldn't be showing live pictures of the attempt to rescue the President and the other hostages lest it gave tactical information to those inside the building.

Jack shook his head. "Fools. Way too early. Some young buck commander trying to make a name for himself has sent in the cavalry. This will end in one of two ways. Dead President or humiliation. I'm taking bets on both."

Kelly gave up with the TV.

"What now?"

"We need to get into town; can you take me?"

In Kelly's silver Ford F-350 they spun out of the lot in front of her auto shop and swung towards town. Cody called Sara again. She picked up for the first ring had finished.

"Did anyone on your level sanction the SWAT team?"

"No. Of course not. We're just as alarmed as you. What are you doing?" her voice was too loud and brittle. The tactical mistake made by the local law enforcement, which had bypassed negotiation and agent protocol was affecting her in the same way it was affecting Cody. It was a monumental screw up.

"They need to pull those officers out of there now."

"I know. That's what we're telling them. God, it's what everyone is telling them. They didn't even get command level clearance to go. Bunch of lunatic mavericks. They think it's High Noon or the Gunfight at the OK Corral. Where are you?"

"Heading into town. We'll be there in...Kelly?"

"Two minutes," Kelly answered, keeping her eyes on the road as the houses around them thickened in number, and the taller brick buildings at the center of Dry Mouth came into view.

"Two minutes," Cody repeated into Kelly's phone. "You're going to need to contact whoever the commander is on the ground and tell him to expect me."

"I will."

"And you're going to have to vouch for me, and send them my ID."

"Because you haven't got any? Great our best guy in the field and no one's going to believe who he is. I'll get on it."

He could hear Sara tapping a few computer keys. "The Secret Service commander, if he isn't one of those idiots Gung Ho-ing into the church is Ray Hacker. Know him?"

"Nope. Get that picture over there fast."

Jack clicked off the iPhone and tossed it onto the dash. Kelly picked it up, looked briefly at the screen, and slipped it into her shirt pocket.

"Who are you, Jack? *What* are you?"

"I'm a government employee…"

"BS, Jack. You're not like any civil servant I know. That number you called had a Washington area code. You're a spook, right? CIA? NSA? Some other shady acronym? What?"

Jack closed his eyes and shook his head. "I really don't need an inquisition now, Kelly. If I'm going to help in any way I can, I'm going to have to focus on what's going on, and that means not focusing on you."

As Cody opened his eyes, he saw Kelly's chin was set and her lips were bloodless. She had done nothing but help him and be welcoming to him since he had had Mike drive him over to her place this morning. He felt a heel. Too many people had been brushed aside and forgotten about since he had joined the service, since he had become what he had become after the death of his family.

Maybe it was time to stop pushing away, and do some pulling in.

"It's not that I won't tell you, it's that I can't. Please understand that what I am doesn't officially exist and just telling you about what I do might make you a target. So, I'm sorry if I came across as harsh there. You didn't deserve that, but I don't know what I'm walking into right now and..."

He hesitated. Kelly's eyes flicked across to him. "...And?"

"And I don't know if I'm going to be walking out again."

* * * * *

The President's face was in the floorboards on the altar. Pavlina's hand was reaching for his across the varnished wood. She was sobbing as the bullets flew and the crazy sheriff had made his break for the door.

Harwood blinked as the bullets flew over his body, and the screams and shouts counterpointed the gunfire.

That idiot sheriff was going to get them *all* killed.

There was no need for anyone to play the hero. The situation would be dealt with by the Secret Service and the law enforcement officers outside the church. They would send in trained negotiators, there would be hostages exchanged for food and water. The women would be allowed out first. There was a whole stream of future options passing through the President's head in a Catherine Wheel of sparking images. Those images immediately told him he was panicking. He found Pavlina's hand and squeezed it as much for her as he did for him.

There was a burst of submachinegun fire from the front entrance of the church, and the President risked an opened eye to look along the aisle to the doors which led into the vestibule. The idiot sheriff was thudding to the ground, dropping his pistol and there was look of pure shock on his craggy face. He'd been shot by the men who had come in behind him.

Behind Kevlar shields with transparent Plexiglas viewing windows, six members of a SWAT team were crammed three abreast in two rows in the doorway, the muzzles of their guns poking between the shields.

"Nobody move!" came the gruff voice from the lead SWAT officer. "That includes the hostages. We don't want to shoot anybody, but if you do move you will be dropped. Stay still and stay calm!"

The President felt a warm glow spreading through his gut. The rescue had begun already, and the stupid terrorists dressed as chefs were going to the gas chamber or be killed where they stood. He begun flicking through the people he was going to fire from the secret service for allowing two of his protection team to be turned against him. He thought about honoring the SWAT team with the highest congressional medals for bravery. He squeezed his wife's hand again and allowed himself a smile. Maybe that idiot sheriff hadn't died for nothing.

He'd distracted the terrorists enough to allow the SWAT team access to the church. Maybe, Harwood thought he should spring for a bravery award for the sheriff too. All of this would be good for his numbers. Coming out unscathed from a hostage situation? That would make a second term a shoo-in. He could probably jettison that loose-cannon VP

Mulray along the way. She was a good shield, but the prayer breakfast gaff had moved her towards the liability section again.

The President realized he was still panicking and tried to quell his thoughts to a more manageable speed.

This wasn't over yet. The hiring and firing and political retribution could wait for now. First thing they had to do was get out of here.

"D...don't...shoot!" The lead chef said. His hands raised in surrender.

The President liked that the scumbag was scared. He liked that a lot. He hoped lead Chef would make a sudden move or not comply so that the brave SWAT team could take him and the other terrorists out in a hail of bullets. If he kept his head down when the firing started, Harwood reasoned, then there would be a good chance the bullets flying around would miss him completely.

Go on, you scumbag...make a move. Go on.

But to the head chief's disappointment, the head chef fell to his knees and raised his hands above his head even higher.

Damn.

"We surrender unreservedly..." head chef whined. "Please don't kill us...please don't..." The whine was thin and weak. Like a toddler trying to stop its mother from smacking its backside for putting its hand too near the fire.

Harwood rolled his eyes. His ribs were hurting against the hard wood of the altar, and his knees ached from kneeling.

Just get this over with so I can get up, he thought.

At first, the sound coming from the head chef's mouth sounded like a sob. A small explosion of air mixed with emotion, but as it continued, and the rasping sound increased volume in his throat, Harwood realized that what he was hearing wasn't a sob, it was a giggle.

It was a giggle that became a full-blown guffaw that echoed around the rafters.

"I'm sorry," head Chef said between gales of laughter, "I tried, I really tried, but I just can't keep it up."

Head chef sighed and dropped his hands, "Do it, boys."

And then without another word, the three SWAT team members at the back of the sextet drew their black bladed combat knives and in one coordinated motion slit the throats of the three team members in front of them.

The men went down gurgling and frothing blood.

The SWAT team members standing, kicked their dying comrades' guns away across the floor, and stepped over their bodies into the body of the church, their mouths smiling and their eyes alight with triumphal fire.

President Harwood dropped his gaze and began panicking again.

CHAPTER 12

"So there *was* a third option then..." Cody said as he watched the bodies of the three dead SWAT members, their uniforms now complemented by bibs of fresh blood, rolled out of the church, to bounce down the steps and slither unceremoniously into the dirt. "More traitors."

Ray Hacker, field commander of the President's Secret Service detail was looking at the picture emailed from Langley and the brief details of Jack Cody.

He looked up in the operations command truck, surrounded by screens, desks at which Intel operatives worked GUIs of constantly moving meshes of data, alongside glass mounted maps of Dry Mouth and surrounding areas. The room was abuzz with chatter, somewhere an alarm went off that was killed on the second wail by an operative who had to suck his knuckles afterwards because he'd hit it so hard.

"I've had two of my security detail kill two of my best agents in front of the President, and I've just lost three SWAT team members to their fellow officers before they threw their bodies out into the dirt – and now you turn up looking like Hobo's nightmare and I'm expected to believe the CIA think you're someone who can help out? Mister Cody, right now I don't know who I can trust. We have been compromised at the highest level, my head is spinning and to be honest, I don't know if I'm a traitor myself."

Four screens on the wall of the truck were showing different angles of the front of the church. The dead SWAT team members lay where they'd been thrown. The doors of the church had closed again and the tension in the room would have blunted a razor.

"Commander Hacker, I can help."

"Maybe you can, but I don't know you from a hole in the ground. None of my operatives know you, and unless I hear from someone I trust—not some Langley email—I'm going to change your clearance. Now, I've got things to do if I'm going to get the President out of there in one piece. Unless you can come up with something more credible than a scanned photograph in an email, you can get back outside the perimeter. Do I make myself clear?"

Jack was escorted from the truck by two agents and walked all the way back to the main street roadblock where Kelly was waiting in the crowd.

"What happened?"

"Red tape happened. Hacker doesn't know which end is up and he wasn't going to take a chance on a guy coming out of the desert with no ID of his own, and no real evidence from

Washington and Langley of who I really am."

"Can't you get that woman you spoke to talking to him again?"

They walked on back through the milling people, who were watching the street towards the church spire, their eyes ago, and their mouths hollows of shock. A credible threat to the institution of the President, and the actual man himself hadn't happened in a very long while. The waves of shock were washing from the ordinary people in the street and washing right up to the truck where Commander Hacker was pulling out his hair.

"There's no point right now. He's not in the mood for listening. And to be honest, I don't really blame him. There are traitors everywhere. Whoever these people are they must have friends in high places for one and have been planning something like this for a while. Secret Service security agents are highly trained and vetted within millimeters of their life. To infiltrate a SWAT team is one thing, and could be done, but the President's secret service detail? That takes influence, money and ideology."

They were away from the glut of onlookers among a group of military trucks and network TV vehicles with satellite dishes on top. Cody looked back along the street. If he didn't know the truth, he would have been amused by the hoopla that surrounded any Presidential visit to a half-horse town like Dry Mouth. The millions of tax dollars being burned before the events had taken a turn for the worse. All because the President wanted to come to a funeral to boost his poll numbers.

The whole thing stank like a dead dog in the hot sun.

"You okay?"

"Huh?"

"You look like a lost little boy," Kelly said with compassion rather than sarcasm.

"I'm not the only one who lost today," Cody said. "We all did."

Shaking his head and stuffing his hands into his pockets he walked back towards Kelly's truck.

* * * * *

Sara tried phoning Jack again, but she was getting no answer.

The Special Activities Center operations room was full of bodies in gaggles of animated conversations and head scratching in front of computer terminals. Strictly speaking, Sara wasn't supposed to be in the operations room, but there was an *all hands on deck* feeling rushing through the building.

Although the CIA was almost exclusively concerned with espionage and their counter measures overseas, there was still a role for them to play in any domestic terrorist incident of this nature. They would be asked for any intelligence that they had that might have given some kind of warning of the attack on the President. They would be expected to know which international terrorist cells might have made their way on the US to carry out this operation, and they certainly would have been asked what they knew about any compromising material foreign governments might have used to turn the agents in the President's security detail.

The lines that existed between international and domestic terrorism were becoming way more blurred than they used to be in the information age. If you were so minded, you could direct an operation like this against the United States from a hovel in Bilal Town, Pakistan—as Osama Bin Laden had proved.

All it took was a laptop, a cell phone and a heart filled with hatred for the Infidel.

Sara had clearance across the building, but she ran agents in the field. All her guys and gals were across the world. The only guy she had on the scene was Jack Cody, and Ray Hacker of the Secret Service was not trusting anyone right now.

There had already been talk among the gaggles of getting a plan together to offer to Hacker and his cohorts in Dry Mouth, where they would offer tactical assistance, and CIA boots on the ground as support to the Secret Service, but no one had given the go order yet. So, Sara was going through screen grabs taken from the film of the caterers who had walked into the church through the ring of Secret Service Agents, National Guard, Marines and Federal Agents.

Jud, Sandra and Bo Elkins had been IDed pretty quickly, as had Henri Charon. Sara knew the story of the battle at their home in New Mexico, and that they had been on the run for the last six weeks. There had been no sightings of them, and that meant they'd been holed up somewhere and they had been given succor by supporters. She could guess the kind of people who would harbor people like Elkins and his clan, but what didn't mesh was the sophistication of this event. This would need military grade intelligence, and it would need a huge amount of seed cash. Money, that when the Elkins had busted out of their ranch, it was thought they didn't have.

So, who was bankrolling this? Who wanted the President held hostage, and who would encourage Elkins to do this?

That was the big hole in the intelligence right now.

As was where the other Elkins child, Tod was right now. He hadn't walked into the church, and as far as the guest list had showed—no one matching his description was among the mourners.

But that might mean diddlysquat too. If whoever had planned this—and she was sure it hadn't been Elkins—they could easily have falsified the mourner manifest.

But...if they could do that for Tod, they could have done it for the others and then they wouldn't have need to take the risk of pretending to be caterers.

Which led Sara to the unhappy conclusion that Tod Elkins was not in the church.

So, where was he?

Sara was levered unceremoniously out of her thoughts as a steaming cup of coffee was placed on the desk in front of her. "Double shot, black, no sugar. Just the way you like it."

Sara turned away from her screen. Analyst Denis Barber, all freckles and unruly hair, tie undone, collar unbuttoned, was standing next to her.

Denis was sweet but a bit obvious. He'd been bringing un-bidden coffees to Sara for a few weeks now, ever since standing next to her at the coffee machine, he'd found out exactly how she liked her coffee.

If not her men.

He was five years younger, had a Boston Irish accent, and she could tell he was drumming up the courage to ask her out for a drink or a movie or both.

It amused Sara a little to be chased by a younger man, but she didn't have the heart to tell him that he wasn't her type.

Too thin. Too young. Too not Jack Cody.

But she liked the coffees, and his wry sense of humor made her smile. "You look frazzled." Denis said. "So I thought I'd bring you some unfrazzling."

"Thanks. Just trying to get my head around all this." Sara picked up the coffee cup and sipped at the edge.

"Tell me about it. I got data up the wazoo and nothing to show for hours of crunching. There will be something here. Somewhere."

Denis' optimism may have been a little naïve, but it was at least endearing. Sara had come to see the Intelligence Analyst more as an affectionate puppy dog, than as future dating potential. But in a fast-moving office of agents and support staff, he was nice to have a round, and he brought coffees as well, so, win.

The phone on the next desk along rang, and as no one was there right now to answer it, Denis leaned over and took the call. He listened for a moment and said. "No, this isn't Agent Durell's desk. Let me transfer you." He put the receiver against his shoulder and stabbing the transfer code for Sara's desk into the keypad told Sara, "For you."

"Who is it?"

Denis shrugged as the phone on her desk buzzed and she picked it up. "Hello?"

"No," the voice was female. "Is that Sara Durell?"

"Yes. Who am I speaking to?"

"I don't want to say my name. And I don't want to say why I'm calling. I need to see you face to face."

The hairs on the back of Sara's neck started to rise. There was an authenticity and veracity to the woman's voice that immediately spoke of truthfulness.

Denis mouthed, "Everything, okay?"

Sara nodded. Denis nodded, smiled *"laters"* and wandered away back to his frazzle-inducing analysis. Sara lowered her voice. "Is this anything to do with what is happening to the President?"

"I can't say. Not here and now. I don't know who I can trust. But I'm scared, and you should be too."

"Why?"

"Because it could mean the end of everything."

CHAPTER 13

It was like a scene from a dime novel.

Sara had left the office and walked to a phone booth on Pennsylvania Avenue, where she found, as directed, a sticker with another telephone number on it, which she had to call from the booth.

The woman had answered on the first ring and gave her an address of a parking garage back in the opposite direction along the Avenue. She wished she'd still had her sweats on as she jogged along the street through the afternoon crowds. Sara reached the garage and had worked up quite a sweat.

She walked past the barrier and down the slope into the underground parking area. It was cooler and less humid down here, and the sweat on her forehead became almost chill as it evaporated. There was a smattering of cars parked under the harsh florescent lighting.

The woman's voice on the phone had told her to go to Bay 5b. There would be a Blue Subaru parked there, and the woman who wanted to speak to her had said she would be there.

Sara had her Glock in her belt holster under her jacket. It would have been stupid to not come armed, especially when the woman initially had told her not to tell anyone they were meeting.

All Sara had done was put a note in her desk dairy that she had an anonymous phone call, and the location of the phone booth she had been sent to. If anything happened to her, her desk diary would at least tell anyone looking into what had occurred, a clue as to where she had gone at least.

There was indeed a blue Subaru parked in bay 5b on this level. There were black puddles on the yellow striped tarmac, which reflected a stuttering fluorescent above it. As the light flickered off the windshield, Sara shaded her eyes to see if she could get a look into the car before approaching.

A hand, feminine and cuffed in a white sleeve waved above the back seat inside the car.

Sara shrugged, and approached, pulling her jacket to one side to make access to the Glock all the easier if she needed it in a hurry.

The hand came up again, a little more insistent this time. Whoever the woman was, she was trying hard not to give away who she was to anyone who might be watching. She appeared to be crouched down deep in the foot well of the Subaru. Keeping her head down. On the telephone as well as sounding authentic and truthful, she'd also sounded pretty scared.

Sara looked around. Apart from the cars dotted around,

she could see no one near. She was now almost level with the front of the Subaru. Like a periscope the hand came up again. This time it wavered rather than waved, and then fell back quickly.

Sara drew her gun.

Suddenly this didn't feel right at all.

The roar of engine noise as a car off to her right started up was joined almost immediately by the squeal of tires on the tarmac.

Sara turned just soon enough to see the hood of a black recent plate Buick Regal bearing down on her in a growling drift as it turned.

Everything was instinct from that moment. Sara didn't think as she rolled, had no plan as she hit the wet tarmac and didn't tell her body to get up onto one knee as the Buick skidded past and headed for the exit from the parking garage.

She did however make the decision to fire three shots into the trunk of the thing. The metal buckled, split and showed silver around the three holes punched into it, but the Buick didn't deviate from its course and skidded into another drift that turned the vehicle through ninety degrees and launched it up the exit ramp.

Two more shots from Sara smashed the side window and the passenger door. But if her rounds had found a human tar-get there was no sign of a deviation in the car's trajectory. It disappeared from view in a spray of dirty water and a squeal of protesting tires.

Sara got up and checking that there were no nearby cars

about to start up and bear down on her, she turned her attention to the Subaru and the hand that had been waving above the back seat.

Sending the gun first and her body second around the Subaru she saw what the hand had been attached to. There was a body of a woman in the backseat, its face a mush of tears, dislodged jaw and blood and flesh torn away to exposed skull around the hairline.

The hand hadn't been signaling to Sara. It had been the confused limb meanderings of a woman who was still clinging to consciousness after a severe beating.

Sara opened the door and the stench of fresh blood was overpowering. She knelt down to the woman's ear and felt for a pulse.

"It's ok, I'm going to get you help."

There was a pulse, and Sara was thankful for at least that. The woman's hand reached for Sara's and her lips quivering around her destroyed jaw tried to form words, but they came out slurred.

"It's ok, don't try to talk. Just let me get help."

Sara tried to let go of the woman's hand, but the injured squeezed harder to hold onto it. Amazingly she shook her head and tried to speak again.

Sara had her cell to her ear and was about to speak to the 911 dispatcher, but this time she did hear the one word the woman amended to enunciate through her smashed teeth before she slipped into full unconsciousness.

"Traitors."

* * * * *

"Traitors" said Brant Stevens.

In the back of the gold plated and diamond encrusted interior of his personal Humvee, the rugged actor was watching the events unfolding at the church in Dry Mouth on one of the small screens dotted around the sumptuous interior of the vehicle.

Brant liked to consider himself a throwback to the movie stars of old. The ones his dad had shown him on the TV when he was growing up. The Tyrone Powers', the Gary Coopers and the Charlton Hestons, real men you could believe in.

Not these namby-pamby new men types with their sensitive eyes and their deep thinking. And not the olive oil covered musclebound so-called hunks of the 1980 and 1990s. Men who looked less the action hero and more the like a guy who'd failed the audition for the Village People.

Brant had made his name playing hard men, in hard situations and doing as many of his stunts as the insurance androids would allow him to.

When he was off duty, you'd never see Brant without a cigar in his mouth, a drink in his hand or a pneumatically enhanced Penthouse Pet on his arm.

That the cigars were fake—he couldn't abide smoking—or the drink was alcohol free, and the woman was paid to be there was neither here nor there. Brant had a brand image to maintain, and he was more than happy to do that.

He'd spent the last three days driving around Arizona

scouting locations for the next film he wanted to make.

His stunt coordinator, Vick Lammy, an ex SAS special forces operative who was now making a very good name for himself on this side of the pond, making action movie stars look great, was on the seat next to him. Watching, enthralled and appalled at what they were seeing on the screens..

Vick ran his hand over his black bald head and blew out his cheeks. "Mofos. Absolute Mofos."

Vick was a bull of a man, with a scar running from his forehead to the edge of his shoulder blade that he said he'd acquired in a knife fight in Syria. He'd been there with his British unit screwing up Russian operations. "Yow should see the other guy," he'd said when Brant had first asked him about the wound.

Vick wasn't pretty, but he sure transmitted an air of confidence that he knew exactly what he was doing and how to do it.

The driver of the Humvee was another of Vick's people. Sharon Phillips was British too, one of the best female stunt operators around—so she'd tell you after a couple of drinks—as well as Brant's Arizona chauffeur.

Sharon was an ex-British army combat instructor who found she could make a ton more money with Vick in Hollywood than she ever could in Jolly Olde England. She was a broad=shouldered woman, with man's biceps, short hair, but generous of smiles and good natured to a tee. Her accent wasn't the cut glass of the upper-class officers she'd spent her career training, she was a hardnosed Cockney from the East End of London.

Vick was what the Brits called a Brummie—he was from Birmingham, England's second city—and his accent, when Brant had first heard it, was like something from another planet. You became *Yow*. Black became *Blick* and the rest of his words would rise and fall in a singsong stream that made him sound he was ex-Disney rather than ex-SAS.

But Brant respected and relied on both, and was happy to do so.

Over the past five years, both had helped catapult Brant's movies into the upper echelons of Action Movie Heaven. The script for Arizona Takedown would be their next triumph he was sure of it.

If only they could find the right setting.

Brant's cell rang. He killed the news on the screen with the remote and answered. It was Con O'Leary, his producer back in California, and the fat, sweaty pile of wobbling flesh didn't sound happy.

"We need to talk. Where are you?"

"You know where I am, Con. I'm in Arizona with Vick and Sharon scouting. Now what do you want?"

"Have you seen the news?"

Brant and Vick exchanged glances.

"Of course, I've seen the news."

"Not about the President, you doofus. About Global."

Global were the company bankrolling *Arizona Takedown*. They were putting up the lion's share of the capital to get the film made on a budget approaching a hundred million dollars. Brant was good business.

"No, I haven't seen the news about Global. I dunno if you've noticed, but someone has kidnapped the President. That's kinda leading the news."

He heard Con sigh. "Brant, Global have gone under. Over-extended on everything, built on sandcastles. There's no money. There's no movie and there's no, as of this moment, Brant Stevens. Your holding in Global is gone too. You're bankrupt compadre. Bankrupt."

CHAPTER 14

As Cody and Kelly walked into the Dry Mouth PD offices it was clear that the chaos on the outside of the building was being equally matched by the chaos on the inside of it.

Mike looked flustered, torn and glad to see them as they came in. There were shouts coming from one corner of the room as a group to men in suits waved their arms around and gesticulated, and over on the other side of the office was another group around a small bald man who Cody thought he recognized but couldn't place the name, and in the middle of it all was a reporter, and a cameraman not knowing which way to point their cameras or microphone.

Mike came over shaking his head. "You try to be nice to people and help them out and look what happens. I've got Governor Kellerman here setting up his base of operations but pissed 'cause there aren't enough telephone lines, and the computers were bought before Noah learned to swim. Over in the blue corner it's the Town Council arguing about the best way to exploit the out of town dollars they think is going to roll into their pockets from all the state and federal employees here trying to clean up the mess in the church, and then there's Brittany Franco thinking she's got the scoop on the whole world because she can see the church from my window, and how I've had CNN, Fox, MSNBC, BBC and uncle Tom Cobbly and all begging me to let them up here so they can get the same view as Brittany. Man, I wish I'd stayed in bed."

Kelly gave Mike a hug and reached up to kiss him on the nose. "You're adorable when you're in a fix, Mike. Don't ever go changing."

Mike rolled his eyes and regarded Cody. "I'm sorry, my friend, we still don't know anything about your brother. I guess that's why you're here, yes?"

"Thanks, they couldn't tell me anything in Secret Service command either. David's got a smart head on his shoulders. I'm sure he'll keep it down."

Mike's face looked confused. "You've been through the line. To speak to the Secret Service? Not even I could get the governor through under that lid."

"He has clearance," said Kelly. "Hush hush on the QT but Jack here's a spook."

"I'm not a spook. And I had clearance. Not any more it would seem. The Secret Service commander doesn't trust his own shadow what with all the turncoats. I was given a polite thanks but no thanks when I offered my...experience."

Mike looked impressed. "I knew you served man, but I didn't..." a thought struck him. "Is that why you're here? That's why you came into town in plain clothes? You knew this was gonna happen? You're like, investigating it?"

Jack shook his head. "Nope. Pure luck. Pure bad luck."

Kelly was helping herself to a soda from a crate of cans which had been cracked open on a nearby desk. She handed one to Cody who took it gladly. He hadn't had anything to drink since the beer, and that was the only liquid he'd had all day. He was starting to feel claggy and slow. The Arizona heat could dry you out like a prune in a matter of hours. He finished the can, and fished another from the crate, enjoying the carbonated bite at the back of his throat.

Now that Mike had told Cody that the small bald man was the governor, Cody could put a name to the face. It was Frank Kellerman. There had been a number of #METOO scandals in his past which normally would have put paid to any political career. But Kellerman also had a surfeit of personality and a homely charm which seemed to get him over the line every election day. He was a survivor, and as Cody watched he saw the way the people in his orbit hung on his every word, even those talking variously into cell phones. There were about eight people around him, and they all had their eyes fixed on him, waiting for their next order.

On the other side of the room, the Town Council were getting into the nitty gritty of their argument. One woman stood out. A tall, raven haired fifty something who was dressed to assassinate. She was pointing her finger in another councilor's face and she was taking "none of his misogyny". According to her, Dry Mouth was going to, "do the responsible thing. They were going to help the President, not think of ways to make a quick buck, and if you ever try to put me down just because I'm a woman again, I'm going to castrate you with a rusty spoon Buster Lyndhurst!"

Jack must have been showing his admiration for the councilor because Kelly whispered in his ear. "Tessa Pearce. Longest serving member of the Town Council and she means it about the rusty spoon. Trust me."

Things had come to a head, in both groups. Kellerman was waving at Brittany Franco, trying to get her attention. Buster Lyndhurst had turned from Tessa Pearce and was also waving at the reporter. "Miz Franco, if you have a moment I'd like to..."

But Brittany and her cameraman were looking agog in entirely the other direction.

Kellerman smiled. "Ah, yes, Brittany, if you'd like to proceed with my interview and statement right now, I'm ready..."

But Brittany and her cameraman were ignoring Kellerman too. As his face fell as far as Lyndhurst's had, the reporter led her cameraman along a route that bisected and alienated each group in turn. She was heading for the door, making sure her mike was on, that her hair was okay, and her suit jacket was smoothed down.

Jack, Kelly and Mike looked to see what had caught Brittany's attention so comprehensively.

"*Son. Of. A. Gun,*" said Mike.

"I've died and gone to heaven," said Kelly.

Jack said nothing.

He wasn't really a movie guy and celebrity had no effect on him whatsoever, but even he knew who Brant Stevens was, and the movie star was walking across the office with a smile like a dozen lighthouses on his face, and eyes that looked into Brittany's camera lens like lasers.

* * * * *

The SWAT team turncoats had taken all the weapons and utility belts from the bodies of the men whose throats they'd cut. They'd taken off their own helmets and tactical vests so they could work faster. Then they'd kicked the bodies out of the building from behind the Kevlar shields.

Jud had enjoyed the notion of making the President and the others believe their ordeal was over and he had surrendered. The look on Harwood's face as Pickles had pulled him and the First Lady back to their feet gave him the most wonderful feeling. Everything was going to plan. They now had the men and the weapons to defend the church against any attack. They had Henri, the bomb and they had the President.

Jud turned to Henri who was still sniffing and sobbing a little against the wall. "Henri, my man. Please stand up."

The look of fear that shadowed Henri's face was a sadistically pleasant feeling too. Jud could get used to this sort of thing. "Don't worry, Frenchy. I'm not going to shoot you. Stand up, my man. Stand up. We've got something to show the President, haven't we?"

Henri got to his feet his eyes downcast. His fingers working anxiously across his belly.

"That's it my man. Now go and see the President and show him our little secret."

Henri nodded, and keeping his gaze down on the floor, crabbed along through two rows of pews until he reached the aisle. Then he walked slowly, as if each step took the effort of lifting a thousand tons.

A shot rang out and the floor split open by Henri's feet. The Frenchman was no longer lifting heavy weights with his feet, he was dancing on air as he leapt into it screaming. As he landed, Bo was laughing and putting his Cobra back into his pocket. "Speed up, Frenchy!" he yelled. "We ain't got all day!"

That's my boy, thought Jud. *A real chip off the old block.*

Henri wasted no more time getting to the altar. He stood in front of President Harwood, his shoulders shaking and his chin on his chest.

"Show him, Henri. Show him now."

Henry opened his jacket and lifted up his shirt. There were gasps from those in the congregation who could see the explosives. Harwood's eyes widened, and the First Lady ran two streaks of mascara down her cheeks to plop off her chin and smudge her jacket.

"You see, here's the thing with a hostage situation," said Jud walking over to the President as if he were sauntering through a city park on a warm summer's day. "Once all the negotiating is done. Which I expect them to start soon, the officers outside will absolutely try to breach the building again. Maybe they'll use frame charges, maybe they'll use stun grenades. They're going to want to keep you alive at all costs. They might try snipers they might try gas—there are all sorts of things in their armory. But I have this."

Jud smiled as he pulled out the detonator from his pocket. "If they come in or hurt any of my family, or it looks like we're going to be overrun, I will press this button, and Henri works his destructive magic all over you. I assure you there's enough high explosive strapped to his body to take us all out, and all of the church too."

The President looked at Jud with a look of pure hatred.

"I know what you're thinking, Harwood. There's a very good chance that they've already bugged the place and are hearing everything we're saying. It is standard operating procedure after all. Now that means I've given away the presence of the bomb, and that I'm holding the detonator. I suppose that makes me their first target when they do come in. But as you can imagine, we've already thought of that possibility, haven't we fellow Pledgers?"

The SWAT team, the agents, Sandra and Bo all nodded and held up their hands.

All seven of them were holding identical detonators to Jud.

Jud laughed again. This was turning into quite a party.

CHAPTER 15

The woman from the back of the Subaru hovered on the edge of death. She'd been stabilized in the emergency room, and after bloodwork, CT scans and brief maxillofacial intervention to affix her broken jaw, she'd been taken to Navy Med, Bethesda ICU in an induced coma because of the swelling around her brain.

Her skull had been fractured in nine places, including the orbits of both eyes. An ear had been torn away from the side of her skull and her nose had been minced. She had lasted three hours so far, and the doctors said if she made it through the next twenty-four, she might have a chance of recovery. Sara was not convinced, and twenty-four hours was far too long for her to wait to find out who the "traitors" were.

Sara had ordered a round-the-clock team inside and outside of the woman's room and asked for the ICU floor to be air-locked at all entrances and exits with guards checking IDs in and out. The beating the woman had taken had suggested whoever had carried it out was not expecting her to live. Perhaps their work on the woman had been interrupted when Sara had come down into the parking garage, and they'd hidden in their car until they decided they were able to attack Sara as well.

FBI forensic teams were going over the Subaru now, and agents were checking CCTV for the Buick Sara had fired on. She fully expected to be told the car that had nearly run her down had been abandoned somewhere, but there might be a chance someone getting out of it might have been caught on camera.

There was no point waiting at Navy Med for the still unidentified woman to wake up and talk. The induced coma had to do its work first, and that would take time. If Sara or anyone was going to find out what the woman wanted to tell, what it was that had nearly got her killed, it was going to take legwork and luck.

There was no ID on the woman, and her face had been so destroyed there was no chance of putting out a photograph in the media. Her fingerprints had been taken but had shown no matches on any database they'd been put through. She was as much a mystery as whoever it was who wanted her dead.

That there was a connection with what was going on in Dry Mouth was clear. It would have been easy for the woman to deny the connection when they were speaking in the first telephone call, but the woman had obfuscated and refused to confirm anything. And she had been right not to, as her attempted murder had proved.

Sara had pulled up on her cell phone incoming call records from the database. The first call had been from yet a different payphone on Pennsylvania Avenue. Agents had gone there to check it out, and any CCTV cameras in the vicinity, but they were not going to report back for a good while. Checking CCTV recordings was painstaking and exacting work. It couldn't be rushed. Too many mistakes could and would be made.

So Sara tried to get in touch with Jack again. Whatever their relationship, and their differences, he was always a good person to bounce ideas and theories off. That Sara was relying on this woman Kelly's iPhone to contact Jack was doubly frustrating. So she decided not to think about what Jack might have been doing in Dry Mouth with a woman called Kelly.

On the screens in the Special Activities Center operations room, the church was still the focus of the world's media attention. Their feeds were coming in silently to three side screens on the info wall. The main screen and attendant feeds were from Secret Service cameras set up by Hacker and his men.

Sara had read reports that Hacker had ordered all security clearances of every officer, marine and agent in the hot zone around the church to be checked and triple checked—and to check the veracity of the clearances of the federal SWAT team as well as his agents. Hacker couldn't risk there being any more turncoats among his teams.

Everyone had to be solid. Sara was still amazed that Secret Service agents had been turned in the way they had. That was not in any way possible under normal circumstances, and it showed a security breach of the highest sophistication.

Sara found her eyes flicking around the operations room. Half the people she knew just by name, a quarter of the people she knew by sight, and a quarter she couldn't place having had any dealings with before. In fact, it was only Analyst Denis Barber and his coffees that meant she had someone here she had any regular contact with, and that was only because he was trying to find the backbone to hit on her. She realized, that in the final analysis, she really didn't know the bones of anyone here. And you could only truly trust someone when you knew them to their bones. Someone like Jack.

Is this what post-Dry Mouth was going to be like? If the President's most trusted bodyguards could be turned against him, what about these people in this room?

What about all the government staffers in Washington?

What about *everybody?*

She shivered, even though the operations room was a steady and comfortable 68 degrees. Sara was looking into the future of the people charged with keeping the country safe.

And for the first time since she joined the agency, she didn't like what she was seeing.

* * * * *

"Hello Mister Elkins. Do you think we could talk?"

The negotiator, a thin balding man in his forties, wrapped in Kevlar, with a black tactical helmet, and holding a shield had come to the bottom of the church steps with a bullhorn.

This was the third time he had tried to make contact in the last three hours. They sent him out in the half hour, regular as clockwork. Jud wasn't stupid enough to stand by a window to see out to the front steps, but there were enough bullet holes in the wall for him to squint through.

"I'm going to leave a radio on the front porch by the door. All you have to do is send someone to the door, open in slightly and bring the radio inside. This will give you direct communication to me. My name is Kevin Challis. I'm a trained hostage negotiator, conflict resolution specialist and de-escalation expert. I have twenty years' experience in hostage situations, and all I want to do is get you and the hostages out of there as quickly and as safely as possible. You have my word that while we're talking no attempt will be made to storm the building. I'm going back now, Mister Elkins. Please take the radio. When you do, I'll take that as a sign you are at least willing to talk to us. I hope to speak to you soon, Mister Elkins."

The bullhorn clicked off and as Jud watched, Kevin walked back to the line of vehicles where the surrounding officers were stationed. If he turned his head slightly, he could see men in uniforms setting up a row of arc lights that would keep the church illuminated through the night.

It was just coming up to 4pm local time. They'd been in the church a full eight hours now. The hostages had been allowed to get off their knees and sit cross legged facing the wall. Jud had ordered the SWAT team to secure their wrists with the tactical zip ties they'd brought in with them.

Tactical Zip Ties were not the common or garden variety that a million YouTube videos showed slacker kids how to escape from in one hard but fluid movement. These babies were thickened reinforced plastic with tough inner core that could not be broken. They didn't have enough of the tactical zip ties for everyone, but they had enough to daisy chain the hostages in groups of ten.

The hostages had been relived to get off their knees even though they were now all connected. It would also stop one individual hostage making a break for it; he or she would have to take nine other people with them.

The President had been allowed to sit back on the altar next to Henri and the First Lady. The reverend, his curate and the two guys who'd come to the funeral were still against the wall on the opposite side of the church to the daisy chained hostages.

Jud scratched his chin as Sandra who had been scribbling notes for him on a piece of paper came over, putting pen through her hair like some damn hippy or something. Jud pulled the pen from her hair as she reached him.

"Don't do that. I don't like it. Act professional. We're in front of the President here."

Sandra smiled and handed Jud the papers. They were waxy and crackly with ink. Jud scanned the lines she had written and nodded with satisfaction. "It's good. Real good. You've done well."

Jud turned to the reverend and the priest and pointed.

"You, your holiness."

Reverend Just started to get up.

"No!" barked Jud. "The other one. You. What's your name?"

"David Cody, sir."

Jud grinned. "You're a fast learner, boy."

David was on his feet now, after helping Reverend Just to get back to the floor on his clearly aching legs. "I'm just like everyone else, sir. I want to get out of here. All of us."

Jud pointed to the main doors into the vestibule. "Well I'd pray a little harder if I were you. But in the meantime, go get the radio from outside the door. I'm ready to parley with the world."

CHAPTER 16

"My fellow Americans, I speak to you today from the Oval Office in a moment of national crisis. We have gone through a door that no one thought would ever be opened. I still have the fervent hope that President Harwood, the First Lady, and all the hostages will be released unharmed from the Arizona Church where they are being held. We have yet to hear anything concrete from the people who have committed this willful act of violence, so we can only guess at what their motivations are. I wanted to explain to you this evening what we are doing to ensure damage to this great nation will not occur as a result of this heinous act. Under the emergency powers granted to me in these challenging circumstances as the Vice President, I have today given orders that all military and service personal are put in a state of highest readiness to respond to whatever additional threat might result from this action—on a day that was supposed to celebrate and memorialize one of the greatest Americans it has been my privilege to know, Jefferson McDaniel, it breaks my heart that we have been presented with the deeds of evil men. As well as putting our brave service personnel on alert, I have ordered that trading be suspended on the Stock Market and other indexes, and that the US Dollar's rate should be frozen on the international exchanges until the present crisis is over. This is a necessary precaution to protect the economy at this time and ensure the continued prosperity of each and every American. We are a strong nation, we are a brave nation, and we will all get through this together. I pray the President will be back soon in this office leading the nation once again. I will make further announcements as necessary to keep you informed of the progress being taken to release the President. Good evening to you all and God Bless America."

"And cut it there," the director said.

As the feed went down and the monitor screen next to the camera flicked to black, Vice President Mulray leaned back in the chair, placing her hands on the Resolute Desk. She skimmed her fingers across the smooth surface as if she were sucking up the strength of its history to pour succor and nourishment to her own veins.

No one in the room spoke until the director and the cameraman finished packing away their gear and the sound man had rolled up his cables. Then the President's secretary ushering them out of the room, clicked the door shut behind her.

Darren Hadrian sat forward expectantly on one of the sofas, where Cortina Lane was scribbling notes onto a pad balanced on his spider thin thigh. Next to them, the Secretary for Defense, the Chair of the Fed, and the National Security Chief were waiting on the VP to speak.

Mulray closed her eyes and sighed. "This is the darkest of days. It's difficult to express hope and optimism in the face of such events. What is the latest from the church?"

"We have made contact through our negotiating team," the National Security chief said. "Elkins is talking, but he's not saying much. We have listening devices in place, cameras and long-range visual access. The President is unharmed..."

"For now," said Mulray gravely. The National Security chief nodded.

"Yes, for now. The other hostages are uncomfortable, thirsty and hungry, but otherwise unmolested. We're raiding the houses of the SWAT teams and the two Secret Service agents who have gone over. We still have no lead on what has happened to Debbie Langwith."

Mulray shook her head and sighed again. "Could it be true? Your suspicions about my DCOS?"

"Her personal computer logs seem to indicate she was either a conduit for information to a group calling itself The Pledge Holders, or one of its leaders. All we have at the moment is that the President's itinerary for today was emailed to a dead letter internet service and accessed by persons unknown at this time. At the very least it seemed Miz Langwith is a sympathizer."

Mulray's face fell. "Langwith was never part of my campaign. Her appointment came through as a recommendation from the President's office. I think it would be prudent to make sure all her bona fides are checked and double checked. And be discreet. I don't want there to be any leaks on this. The American people are reeling from today's events, the knowledge that someone at the very highest level of the government could in some way be involved is not only troubling—it will destroy all confidence in this administration. We cannot allow that to happen."

"Yes, Madam Vice President, I concur," said the National Security chief.

The Oval Office became quiet again. Mulray pulled a tissue from a box on the desk and dabbed at the corner of her eye. "I have no idea what will happen next, but I think things may get worse before they get better, and if that is the case, God help us all."

Jack couldn't believe that Kellerman was even thinking about the idea.

Even though Jack was on the periphery of the conversation, he'd picked up enough of the crazy plan Brant Stevens was pushing to the governor to be very worried indeed. He hadn't interjected yet, he was biding his time, but the urge to say something when a concrete decision was made was building up in him. There had already been a number of ejections from the room and Cody didn't want to be one of those just yet, but it was becoming harder and harder to sit on his own mouth.

Brittany and her cameraman had been unceremoniously removed from the Dry Mouth PD office with much protesting about the *freedom of the press* and their *right to know what was going on* so they could transmit it to the people of America. Kellerman had told her that he would be making a statement to her outside the Dry Mouth PD office in due course, and she would have to take that or leave it.

Tessa Pearce had been asked to leave soon after, at the insistence of Buster Lyndhurst because she *couldn't be trusted not to blabbermouth all over* Dry Mouth. Tessa had protested as much as Brittany but had still been ejected so that Brant Stevens could make his pitch to Kellerman in what he called a "positive and patriotic atmosphere".

Mike had looked pained to implement Kellerman's orders to remove both the press and Tessa Pearce but had carried them out all the same. As Kellerman had explained to him, as governor he was the ranking law enforcement officer in the room, and Mike was duty bound to follow his instructions. Mike was in a bind, but he was not going to risk his job or his pension.

Jack and Kelly had been allowed to stay because they hadn't as yet, gotten involved, and Kellerman and the others hadn't taken any notice of them because they were keeping themselves to themselves.

"You don't like this do you?" Kelly whispered to Cody.

"No. It stinks," he replied. "It's crazy, but crazy never put a politician off making a name for himself."

When the room had been cleared to Stevens' satisfaction,

he'd introduced Vick and Sharon to the others, he'd emphasized that they were stunt performers second, and combat veterans first. The SAS, he'd said, were comparable in skill and ability to Navy SEALs. They had the brains and the brawn to carry out what he was suggesting, but above that, they could be trusted.

"Look at what's happened here, Governor Kellerman – Secret Service agents and federal SWAT teams have become terrorists. The government response has been woeful; they've been like a rabbit in the headlights. They're out there now negotiating with a present and credible threat to the institutions of this great country. Someone should be doing something more active to bring this situation to a close. And if the government won't do it, then maybe the governor can."

Kellerman's eyes had lit up at this suggestion. Cody had seen that the idea appealed to the man's political mind first and foremost. Not to any compassionate notions he had about rescuing the President or the other hostages. Cody saw the calculations going on behind Kellerman's eyes.

"You think you can do this?" Kellerman had asked.

"Yow bet we can," answered Vick emphatically. "We can neutralize the bad guys with extreme prejudice. All we'll need is some equipment, some tactical gear and Bob's yer uncle."

Jack knew the reputation of the SAS was high around the world. They were brave, determined and skilled fighters in any theater of war. They had led many raids in the gulf covertly. They knew what they were doing. But this was still insane.

Sharon had piped up, "We have six men en route here already," she looked at her wristwatch. "Wheels down in ninety minutes. Then an hour from the airfield to Dry Mouth. They're bringing the equipment we'll need, and they'll be ready to go within two hours of arrival."

"More stunt men?" Lyndhurst asked.

Brant shook his head, "No…what you might call soldiers of fortune who are always in readiness for operations of a sensitive nature. Mercenaries yes. But good, solid men who will relish the chance to neutralize Elkins and his family."

Kellerman was still calculating. "And who picks up the tab for this?"

Always the bottom line with these guys, thought Cody.

"I do," said Brant. "My gift to a grateful nation."

"A gift to his public relations team more like," Cody whispered to Kelly. "Even if they fail—which they more than likely will—Brant's going to be able to say he tried, and that's going to be currency for him for the rest of his life."

Kelly squeezed Cody's arm. "But the government aren't doing anything, are they? Negotiating with terrorists. When did that become a thing?"

"If I were Hacker, I would be too. They will be making plans for a hard assault on the church. But you have to keep Elkins and his clan talking. Buy some time. If Stevens' plan is given the go ahead by Kellerman, then I think we're going to have a massacre on our hands."

CHAPTER 17

"Extra pepperoni, Dad, tell them I want extra pepperoni."

Jud held a hand up to silence Bo and spoke into the radio. "And we want extra pepperoni on two of the pizzas."

"And a chocolate milkshake. Double thick." Bo grinned.

"And double thick chocolate milkshake," Jud repeated.

"Ok I got all that," Kevin Challis' voice came from the radio. "We'll have them with you as soon as we can."

"Mightily obliged, Kevin; put it on the President's tab."

Bo and Sandra laughed.

Harwood shifted his position where he was sitting on the altar and Pickles pointed the SIG at his head. "Stay still."

"I am staying still. My ass is numb."

"Like your head!" Bo said. He was warming to the situation considerably. Enjoying, Jud could see, the power that he was able to exercise over someone like the President. Bo was no longer a little cog in a huge machine. All their names would go down in history, and Bo liked that idea. His confidence was shining through. It made Jud proud to see his son blossom in this way.

"Can I have an update on the health and wellbeing of the hostages, Jud?" crackled Kevin from the radio. "We know that you have diabetics there who will need access to insulin and their medication. Maybe they can come out when we deliver the pizza? We don't want anyone suffering unnecessarily, do we?"

"This is necessary suffering," said Jud. "We're medicating the country."

"I'm only thinking of the people in the church Jud, you know that. I'm just concerned."

"And I know all you're concerned with is getting the President out of here, Kevin. You'll spin me any line to get some leverage. Don't try to appeal to my compassionate nature. I don't have one. Get the food here stat, or you won't have diabetes on your mind anymore."

"Jud, I'm sorry I didn't mean to..." Kevin's placating tone drew a wink from Jud to his wife.

"Shut up, Kevin. Just know this. We'll be making a statement about our demands soon. We'll let you all know why we're doing this and what we want to achieve. But first we want us some pizza and some milkshake. Better send some diet soda for the diabetics."

Jud clicked the radio off and joined Pickles at the altar, pulling him away from Harwood and the first lady's earshot.

"Anything?"

Pickles reached into his pocket and pull out his smartphone and thumbed the screen. "Last message was an hour ago, nothing since then. Don't make the statement before eight AM tomorrow morning. We're to keep this going until they give us permission to speak."

Pickles turned the screen to Jud so he could read the message that had been sent to them over secure and encrypted lines of communication.

"Tomorrow is the fourteenth day of the eighth month, and at eight AM you know what that means to our movement. You can speak to the nation. We must hold out until then. You will make all of us proud, Jud Elkins. You are doing a wonderful thing for our country and the world."

Jud licked his lips. He was onboard with the ideology; he was on board with the mission, and he was on board with the plan. But the longer this went on, the more doubts had begun to nibble at the edges of his confidence. He wasn't going to show it to his wife or his sons, or the President, but he still felt the worry inside. "But what if they attack before then?"

Pickles shook his head. "They won't. They will know about the bomb; they will know about the detonators. There is no way they can take us all out at once and they won't want to sacrifice the President to a botched operation. And I'm guessing they still don't know who they can trust outside the church. We're golden, Jud. We're golden."

Jud nodded and walked away from Pickles, jumping down off the altar and going to the pew where he'd left the radio. He picked it up and spoke into the mic. "Oh, and, Kevin?"

Kevin came back immediately, "Yes, Jud? Have you considered my request to let the diabetics go at least?"

"No. Of course not. Easy on the jalapeños. They make my guts ache."

Sara showered at the office and pulled out a change of clothes from her locker, for when she'd dried off.

She'd been in the bathroom splashing water on her face when she'd noticed the grime from the parking garage floor on her jacket arm. When she'd looked down, she'd see the tear in the side of her skirt, and the ladder in her stockings. She'd never considered herself a clotheshorse, but she'd suddenly felt the exhaustion of the day wash through her in a black wave. She was used to working around the clock to get things done, but a shower and a change of clothes would liven her up and make her feel back in focus.

She'd been in dangerous situations before and having someone try to kill her was a rare, but not unknown experience. Still the effect of coming a hair's breadth from death was something she couldn't just push from her mind as she stared at herself in the mirror, dirty and hair awry. So, she'd gone down to the basement to take a shower and get into fresh clothes.

The locker room was deserted. Everyone in the building it seemed was working hard to uncover any information that would lead to a safe conclusion to the situation in Dry Mouth.

She really needed to speak to Cody, to see what his assessment of the things were there now. All she'd been getting was what had been coming in from the news networks. Hacker had been given permission to stop transmitting tactical information to this office in case it got into the wrong ears.

Sara and the people she worked with had smarted at the notion they were not trustworthy, but they kind of understood. Everything right now was on a need to know basis, and on the orders of the National Security Service chief the CIA didn't need to know. They were to continue to look into foreign connections to Elkins and his Pledge Holders, but that was to be the extent of their work until told otherwise.

Sara toweled her hair dry with one hand while she opened her locker to take out her spare suit.

That's when she heard the footsteps behind her.

The locker rooms were open to everyone in the building, so it was not unusual to be in there at the same time as anyone else. What as unusual was that the footsteps were behind Sara, and they were speeding up.

She turned just in time as the tire iron swung through the air and crashed into the locker denting the metal and jarring the arm of her ski-mask wearing attacker. Sara brought a knee up, hard into the attacker's gut. The figure *ooofe*d but didn't go down. The tire iron swung savagely towards Sara's chest and she took a step back as it scythed across her body, catching in the fold of her robe. It had scratched her flesh beneath in a coruscating line, but the impact of the blow had been minor. Sara caught her assailant's arm under her right armpit and shot the heel of her left hand up to connect with the assailant's chin.

Their head snapped back, but the tall figure, in ski-mask and nondescript boiler suite just shook its head and pulled the tire iron away from Sara's body, preparing to bring it down in a two handed strike that would do to Sara exactly the same thing it had done to the woman in the Subaru.

Sara sidestepped and tried to hook a foot behind the attacker's knee. This only half worked. It destabilized the attacker just enough to deflect the blow from Sara's head onto her shoulder. The stunning starburst of pain that exploded as the tire iron connected took Sara's breath away. She only just managed to drop her knees to roll with the blow as best she could. She staggered backwards and the attacker came at her again.

The tire iron whistled down again and again as Sara dodged and ducked. There were only going to be so many times she was going to be able to do this. She had to be perfect every time. The attacker only had to be lucky once.

The tire iron crashed into the metal locker by Sara's ear. The attacker was getting closer, and Sara was tiring of playing duck and dodge. The rear wall of the locker room was coming up fast to her back and she was being pushed closer and closer to a corner where she was going to become easily trapped and a perfect target.

She had to do something to change the dynamic.

Sara shucked off her robe as the iron sped by again. Wrapping the toweling around her hand she flicked it out and missed the attacker, because he stepped sideways. The second time she flicked the robe it wrapped about the descending arm and caught.

Sara yanked the robe.

Twisted in the material the attacker fell forward and got another crunching punch to the belly which hit with such force that it sent a jagged line of pain through Sara's wrist and up her arm.

Sara kept on yanking, and with a roar of triumph she felt the attacker let go of the tire iron, and it clattered to the floor, twanging off the base of a metal locker.

Sara dived desperately for the tire iron. She knew she had to reach it first. Her arm clasped the warm metal, hot from the attacker's hand, and she rolled over, holding the tire iron out in front of her like Excalibur pulled from the stone. Her eyes squinting from the pain in her shoulder, and her breath coming in ragged bursts as she tried to ready herself for the onslaught to come.

A door slammed.

Sara was pointing the tire iron at empty air.

CHAPTER 18

The Soldiers of Fortune as Stevens had described them arrived at the Dry Mouth PD a little after 11pm. They were a
motley crew of Americans, Australians, British and Russian.
They were all built like steam trains, and they were ready for
a fight. The men were each carrying gun bags and rucksacks
stuffed with equipment, and it looked like they certainly had
the tools of their trade on hand. While Vick and Sharon took
them to a corner well out of earshot of the others for briefing,
Kellerman and Brant shook hands and slapped each other on
their backs.

"Governor Kellerman, this is not going to go well for you."
Cody had seen enough. He now reasoned that being here in
the room to listen to what was going on was not as useful
as telling Kellerman a few home truths and possibly getting
himself ejected like Brittany and Pearce.

Kellerman's sweaty jowls clamped tight, and Brant chewed
on his cigar.

"Deputy Wilson, would you kindly ask your friend here to butt out of our business?" Brant said. "In fact, isn't it past his bedtime?"

Kellerman laughed.

Mike held up a hand to Cody and took him to one side. "Jack, I know you have reservation about this, I've seen your face falling harder than a cow chip into a canyon, but these guys seem to know what they're doing. The authorities are doing nothing but appease and talk. You've seen the stuff on the news. At least this gives the President and the others, including your brother, a fighting chance."

"Busting in on a hostage situation isn't like it is in the movies, Mike."

"I know that..."

"But Brant and Kellerman don't. This is all being set up for publicity and glory. You know that. I know that."

"Maybe glory has been a bit in short supply around this great nation for far too long," said Brant coming over. "I don't know who you are, son, but you'd better leave the doing to the professionals. Time for lame-ass snowflakery is over."

Kelly put her hands on her hips, "Jack is a professional, Mister Stevens, you might not know this about him but..."

Jack caught Kelly's eye and shook his head. "I'm off duty and I'm just a concerned citizen."

"Off duty from what?" Kellerman asked, suddenly getting interested. "Who do you work for?"

"Right now, I don't work for anyone, Governor. I'm a visiting friend of Mike and Kelly here, and I'm grateful for the opportunity to sit here in the office and drink Mike's sodas. But I gotta tell you, that what Stevens and you are proposing is foolhardy and dangerous."

"And you'd be an expert, I take it?" Brant said, moving his unlit cigar around his mouth as he spoke.

"I have certain experience in these matters, yes. But all I want to tell you is that going in mob handed like this is going to get people killed. People like the President. I don't think that's going to endear you to a grateful nation."

"Oh no?" said Kellerman.

"No," Cody replied.

"Well you'd better make sure you keep your expert opinions to yourself," said Brant, taking out his cigar and pointing the wet end at Cody's nose. "Because it's men like you who stop this country doing what it should. Vick!"

From the gaggle of mercenaries, Vick looked up.

Brant continued stabbing his cigar at Cody. "Secure this fella here. He's suddenly become a security risk."

Vick pulled a Colt 1911 Government from inside his jacket and pointed it at Cody.

Jack raised his hands.

Vick and Sharon left the group of fighters and came towards Cody. Sharon was reaching into a small bag she was carrying and brought out a pair of police issue handcuffs. Cody was too far from the exit door to make a break without presenting his back as a clean target. The mercenaries were also getting interested. Their heads swiveling to take in Cody and what was going down.

Vick reached Cody, the muzzle of the pistol two feet from the center of Cody's chest.

Vick smiled, revealing a front incisor which had been replaced with a gold tooth. "Now, are we an' thee going to do this the easy way or the hard way, bab?"

✳ ✳ ✳ ✳ ✳

Sara ran into the muggy Washington night. She didn't dare look back until she was two blocks from the building, and even then it was only a glance to see if she could pick up anyone who was following. When she'd not spotted anyone, she sprinted off again, sticking to gloomy side streets and alleys.

In the locker room, she'd quickly dressed, retrieved her Glock from her locker, and hightailed it out of the building without another thought.

Whoever had attacked the woman in the Subaru could get into the CIA building and attempt to kill her, it was a terrifying thought. A more unpleasant thought however followed that one—what if the attacker had been in the building already? What if he or she were an employee of the CIA? What if the influence of the Pledge Holders, whoever they were, stretched as far as the people she worked with?

Sara knew that if they were out to get her, that the first place they would look after the building she worked in would be the apartment she rented in North Washington.

So, she wasn't going there.

She stopped at an ATM and withdrew five hundred dollars from her checking account. Cash was less traceable in the short term than credit, and if the attacker was CIA then there was a good chance they had the ability to access details of her transactions and trace her physical location that way.

With the money slipped into the inside pocket of her jacket—her purse was still in the office—she sprinted off again into the falling night. Streetlights were starting to come on and the air was starting to chill a little, which she was grateful for. She stopped in a small clothing store to buy a plain black overcoat to cover the suit she was wearing, and a Redskins baseball cap, stuffing her hair up into it. Short of buying a false beard this was the best she was going to be able to do to disguise her appearance. In an electronics store she bought a cheap burner phone. Transferring the contacts from her smartphone to it, and after hiding the switched off smartphone in a hedge, under a stone where she could pick it up later if needed, she stopped jogging, and walked on, trying to look inconspicuous.

Sara knew that any calls in or out of Dry Mouth were likely to be monitored by the NSA. If there was a leak there, then just trying to contact Jack, or indeed anyone, would give away her location and compromise the burner.

The time might come where she was forced to use the phone, but right now this wasn't it. She was alone in the capital and right now she couldn't be sure who if anyone she could trust.

Except Jack.

She walked for an hour north west along Clara Barton

parkway overlooking the Potomac to her left. There wasn't a lot of traffic on the river, but the American Legion Memorial Bridge had its usual cargo of cars and trucks, their headlights cutting into the new night, glittering across the surface of the water. She would constantly check the vehicles going by her to make sure she wasn't being tailed.

At the moment nothing seemed to be sticking to her. The only people who came past her were joggers or people having an evening tryst or two. Lovers kissed on a bench as she passed. Other people were walking dogs. Normality reigned.

But normality was the last thing she was feeling. She needed a plan of action.

Firstly, she had to stay safe and out of reach of whoever wanted her dead.

Then she had to find out why they wanted her dead, and who they were.

Why they wanted her dead was possibly the easiest thing to guess at. They must know that the woman in the Subaru had survived and there was a chance that she had said something to Sara.

They couldn't possibly know that the only word that had made it to Sara's ear had been "*traitors*", but they'd want to be sure nothing was getting out. It followed that whoever was behind this was possibly as paranoid as Sara about the people around them. It meant they had something to lose. Positions of power or influence perhaps. How high up the chain did this go?

Sara hugged herself as she walked, the temperature dropping as the cloud cover of the day that had produced so much of the city's humid atmosphere had moved away to the east. She'd need to eat something soon, just to get some fuel into her belly. The night was not shaping up to be exactly bitter, but she'd need to be sharp and nourished if she was going to be able to be at the highest level of alertness.

She was just about to think about where the best and most inconspicuous place to eat was, when the boom of a massive explosion rolled across the city. Sara turned just in time to see a blooming fire cloud light up the horizon, and the plume of smoke that followed it, being forced into the air over the capital.

CHAPTER 19

Jack sat on the cot in the Dry Mouth PD cell. It was a cell in name only, truth be told. Because the story above the library had been converted into the Police Department, the cells were three iron bar cages which had been put into a storeroom at the back of the building. There was no window, and there was only one door leading out of the room.

Jack was still handcuffed, but they'd not tied his feet. He could hear a murmur of voices outside the room but couldn't pick up anything of note. Preparations would be continuing apace, he was sure. Brant's Dirty Half-Dozen were, from what he'd seen before he'd been put in the cage, raring to get going on their ill-advised rescue mission.

If Jack was going to do anything to prevent them he was not only going to have to get out of the handcuffs, the cage, but then he'd have the added problem of getting past whoever was left in the Dry Mouth PD office once the mercenaries had left.

"Well, I'd better get started," Cody said to himself, "can't sit around here doing squat all night."

Jack leaned forward on the cot, and reached down to his boot heel, turning his foot up as he did so. With a small click, the side of the heel clicked open, and a small tray of tools slid out on a concealed spring.

The boots had been a present from Sara, and they had come in useful before. Cody knew if ever he was in a position to lock someone dangerous up, he'd not just take away his prisoner's belt and shoelaces, but he'd have their boots first of all.

In the tray was a thumbnail compass, a razor blade, a tight-ly wound length of paracord, a needle and three lock-picks of various design.

Taking the picks from the tray and sliding it back into his heel, Jack was out of the cuffs in less than eight seconds. But he didn't take the cuffs off completely. He left one cuff on his wrist, and ready to be reattached to the other in case the door to the cell cages opened, and he had to make like he was being a good boy.

The cage entrance was a little trickier to pick with the tools—it took thirty seconds. Cody slipped himself out of the cage, pushed the door closed behind him and stepped towards the door.

If anyone came in now it would be embarrassing, but at least he would have the element of surprise.

He put his ear against the door and listened.

The voices were louder, but still indistinct. But what he also heard were footsteps coming towards the door.

Dammit. He couldn't afford to be seen now.

Jack squeezed himself back against the wall by the side of the door and waited. The footsteps reached the door, and a hand was place on the handle. He braced himself, ready to explode into whoever's face it was behind the door.

But the door didn't open.

Someone in the office beyond shouted, "Holy Hell and Mother of God! Look at that!" It might have been Kellerman. Cody couldn't be sure.

The person outside the door hesitated, let go of the handle and Cody heard the footsteps receding. The voice of a reporter on a TV came on, and the volume was turned up loud.

"We're getting reports of a massive explosion in the capital just after nine PM Eastern Standard Time. Pictures on Twitter from eyewitnesses show that the whole top floor of the Walter Reed Medical Center is ablaze. Speculation is rife that this could in some way be connected to the plight of President Harwood, now entering his twelfth hour of captivity in Dry Mouth Community Church."

The voices on the other side of the door were expressing shock and some outrage. The TV was cut off. Brant's voice rose above it. "Well, there we have it, guys. Proof if proof were needed that the government is paralyzed and the country is under threat in a way it hasn't been since nine-eleven. Let's get this done!"

Jack heard the tramping of feet out of the offices as the mercenaries and, he presumed Brant, went out with them.

It was now he had to take his chance. He would have to

get to Hacker and warn him about what was about to happen.

Jack tensed himself, drew in a breath, and put his hand on the door handle.

Now or never.

* * * * *

Brant was ecstatic as he followed Vick and the others out of the Dry Mouth PD office, down the iron steps at the back of the building, and out into the yard.

Kellerman was just the kind of fool he needed to have got on board. A typical politician with a typical blind spot over his own self-promotion that was easy to manipulate. It had been the easiest acting job Brant had ever had to accomplish, to make Kellerman think all the glory and the plaudits for approving and planning this operation were going to go to him.

Sure, Brant would go along with the story that the governor, beside himself with worry, and not able to trust any of the federal forces, had spoken to Brant and asked him what he could do to help. Sure, Brant would confirm that it was all Kellerman's idea, and that he'd been told that the approval for the raid had been given at the highest level in the government. As at least if all went wrong, Brant would have plausible deniability for the whole scheme. He was just an actor after all with some shady friends with military experience. He was just the middleman after all. But if everything worked out, as Vick had assured him that it would, then Brant would be a national hero for real. The collapse of Global Pictures would be a footnote to his story, and the money would roll in. Enough to keep him in movies for the rest of his life.

Hell, he might even make enough to set up his own studio, and he'd never have to rely on production money ever again. He would finance his own films, in which he would star.

Vick's men had hired their own Humvee at the airport and driven it to Dry Mouth. Down in the lot outside the Police Department, they were checking their gear over and putting on their tactical vests. To anyone passing who didn't pick Brant out from the others, the group of men milling in and around the Humvee would assume they were part of the Secret Service or federal agents getting ready to go towards the church to bolster the forces there.

Once inside the Humvee, a little cramped now that it held nine people, Vick gave the order to drive out of the town and circle north to approach the church on a road he figured would not be as guarded as the roads in town.

Vick's assumptions proved correct. They came from the west onto a two car National Guard roadblock stopping and turning traffic around on the highway.

The Humvee inched up to the block, and a Guardsman came forward companionably. There were three other Guardsmen back behind the SUVs, but they looked bored and tired. They had obviously been there much of the day.

Brant watched as Vick slid the passenger side window down and showed him the pass Kellerman's people had acquired for them. It wouldn't take a lot of scrutiny by anyone with their head in the game, to see that the pass, although official, was just to get someone into the governor's office in the Capitol Complex in Phoenix, but the pass wasn't meant to get them through the roadblock. It was just to keep the hands of the Guardsman busy, while the mercenaries readied themselves.

The young Guardsman squinted at the card as it was placed in his hands—as he looked down, all the doors on the Humvee flew open, and black clothes figures swarmed out.

Vick kicked his door open, and the Guardsman went down like a sack of potatoes. Within four seconds the Guardsmen on the other side of the roadblock were locking down the barrels of six H&K Mp5s and they were raising their hands.

Vick got out of the Humvee and helped the young Guardsman to his feet. "No offence, mate," he said. "Believe me we're not the bad guys here. Have a look at who's in the back on yon car."

Brant leaned forward and waved to the Guardsman. The fleeting moment while his recognition caught up with his eyes made Brant grin. "Don't worry, son. We're just gonna tie you up for a while, and when we get back, I'm going to give you all my autograph."

The young Guardsman nodded. "I...my mom...she loves you, man. She has all your movies."

"Glad to hear it. And I can't wait to make the next one. Might even make you one of the star characters."

"Secure them!" Sharon called to the men in the team.

Once the Guardsmen were all tied up and their weapons loaded into the back of the Humvee and their radios smashed with the butts of their guns, Brant and the others drove the Humvee around the roadblock and headed into Dry Mouth.

CHAPTER 20

It was a risk taking the taxi north from the Potomac to Navy Med. But she had to see for herself. The cab driver she'd hailed had already said no to going to the area around the explosions and fire. It wasn't until she'd promised him a fifty-dollar tip that he'd relented. Even though, as they made their way across town against the flow of traffic, the driver had complained noisily that he was going to get stuck in the streaming away from the hospital. "Look lady. Keep your fifty dollars. I'm gonna lose that just crawling back nose to tail. You'd better get out here. Just pay me what's on the meter."

How Sara wished she could flash her ID, tell the driver it was a matter of national security and that she was commandeering his filthy cab, that smelled of old onions and fresh sweaty feet, to drive her to Navy Med. But as she was trying not to be found until she was ready to be found, that wouldn't be the most prudent of actions. She briefly toyed with hijacking the cab—she still had her Glock after all—but then decided against it. The cab driver was just trying to make his living, and did she really need to go to the hospital to see it for herself?

Sara couldn't answer that question right now. So, she got out of the cab and she walked the last two miles towards the burning building that was lighting up the skyline ahead.

When she got there, a sizeable crowd was gathered across the highway. She stood as near as the police and fire department would allow and felt her heart sinking by the yard.

The whole top story of the hospital was an all-consuming conflagration. The sky was lit up carnival orange, and the sound of the crackling fire, and exploding glass, cut across the night in an evil whisper. She couldn't even guess at the numbers of people who might have died or been injured by the blast. From her memory of the internal geography of the place, the ICU where the woman from the Subaru had been in her induced coma would now be so much burning wreckage and blackened rubble. Hoses were being trained on the flames from a near dozen directions and the Washington fire department did their best to save what they could of the rest of the hospital. Men and women, some doctors and nurses, some in uniform, others in their pajamas and nightgowns were streaming along the road, herded by police officers. Some looked completely untouched by the disaster, others were bleeding from cuts to their bodies and limbs. Some had faces dulled by soot and/or powdered by concrete dust. Others were being pushed in wheelchairs, some on gurneys, and others were simply being carried as the hospital was evacuated.

The people watching the hospital burn were mostly quiet, their eyes bright and shining, reflecting the light of the flames. They were being kept back behind a line by cops who looked just as bewildered and shocked as the members of the public around Sara. Media trucks were drawing up, reporters and camera operators setting up their equipment. Lights coming on, blasting Sara's eyes with their sudden harshness.

Sirens blared from several areas at once. Ambulances coming in, and others leaving in a constant stream. It was a scene that at once felt horribly familiar but also alien. Being here in the midst of it was disconcerting, but at least the anonymity of being in the crowd gave her some sense of security that she wouldn't be spotted by anyone who might be looking for her.

Sara felt her hand falling involuntarily on the burner in her pocket. She almost pulled it out, almost wanted to make a call to someone—anyone—to be reassured that everything was going to be okay. She'd never felt so dislocated and separated from everything she knew and held dear right now. A maudlin sense of dread that hung around her head like the smoke pouring into the sky from the burning hospital.

How far were these people prepared to go? Sara thought, the back of her throat thick with bile. *All this to get rid of one witness.*

If they would send CIA agents to kill her in her own building, if they would hold the President hostage and threaten to kill him—and they would blow up a damn hospital full of sick people, what other lines would the cross?

And what was their ultimate aim?

Sara shook and put her hands into the pockets of her over-coat. She had no worries about the night being chill now. The gusts of heat coming off the burning hospital were rolling over the crowd that had gathered at the intersection. The air was bitter with grit and acrid soot.

It felt like America was burning.

Perhaps it was.

* * * * *

Now or never.

Jack pulled open the door and sprinted from the storeroom that held the cell cages.

The group of councilors around Lyndhurst, Kellerman and his people, Mike and Kelly were gathered around the TV, variously looking from the screen at the DC disaster, out of the window to the church.

Jack made it halfway across the office towards the door before anyone saw him. One of Kellerman's hangers on shouted "Look out! He's escaping!" and everyone spun around and saw Cody haring between the desks.

"Stop him!" Kellerman shouted at Mike. "Shoot him if you have to. That's an order."

Jack was peripherally aware that Mike was pulling his weapon, and flinched, but the policeman, caught in the cleft between his orders and his conscience put a bullet in the ceiling rather than in Cody's body.

Can't stop, I'll thank you later. Cody thought as he made it to the double doors and crashed through them out onto the iron stairs.

He leapt down four at a time, holding onto the railings, and skidding himself around the two turns. Once he was near enough to the ground, Cody jumped over the rail, hit the gravel in the yard, bent his knees, parachute rolled up onto his feet and was away around the corner into the street before the shouts behind him in the building could turn into shots.

The main street of Dry Mouth still had its share of people, but they had thinned considerably since the afternoon. Without a clear view of the church, it was difficult to maintain their interest, it would appear, so they'd wandered back to their homes to watch the two national emergencies unfold on their TVs.

Jack jogged parallel to the roadblock. There was no point trying to get through there. He had no ID, and if Hacker was worth his salt, he'd have given copies of his photograph from Langley to all the Guardsmen on the roadblocks precisely for the reason of looking out for him.

A side street between a bank and a diner came up ahead and he slipped through it. Jogging through the warm night, Cody came up to the corner of the bank, and looked down the utility access road that ran along parallel to main street. A National Guard Tahoe was parked across the road as was being leant on by two Guardsmen who didn't exactly look alert. They were a good thirty yards away so there was no way of coming up to them without being seen.

Jack looked up.

Okay.

Worth a shot.

There was a fire escape from the third floor, which ended in a security ladder which was supposed to be out of reach, but on the other side of the alley was the diner. There was a fire escape attached too, but the catch on the bottom of its security ladder had slipped or broken, and three rungs hung tantalizingly near enough for Cody to jump up and catch.

His fist caught the metal rung and the ladder, protesting as little slid down. Not waiting to see if the Guardsmen or anyone else had heard, Cody began to climb. When he reached the second level, he pulled the ladder back up, and continued up the iron steps to the fire escape on the third level. Apartments or offices above the diner were quiet, and the windows were dark. Either everyone had gone home for the night or were still out in the street trying to catch a glimpse of the action.

Jack put a foot on the railing and boosted himself up, so that his elbows could dig into the tarred felt on the roof of the building. He swung up his legs and rolled flat. The roof of the building above the diner was dotted with air conditioning vents and little else. The surface of the roof that had baked all day in the Arizona sun was still hot to the touch, and Cody felt the warmth radiating into his body as he lay there catching his breath.

He got up in a crouch and looked about. The buildings on the other side of main street were just as tall as the diner and bank, and the buildings beyond. If anyone was watching from the windows opposite, Cody would be seen. He scanned the windows left and right, most of them, because they were commercial properties were dark at this time of night, and behind those where the lights were on the rooms seemed empty.

Jack looked at the gap between the diner and the bank. It was about fifteen feet. It was a jump he could make in his sleep with the right run up. He crawled back along the roof twenty-five feet, stood in a crouch and centered himself for the jump.

One.

Two.

Three...

"There he is!" came a ragged shout across the night. "Get him!"

A bullet tore into the roof at his feet, tearing up the felt, and clanging shrapnel into a nearby air-conditioner vent. It was followed by another. This one zipped past his thighs and smacked into the roof three feet away.

And so, Cody realized, he had no more time to think.

He began to run.

CHAPTER 21

"You know I don't want to antagonize you, Jud, but you know that's impossible." Kevin's voice pleaded from the radio. It was near midnight, and the next phase of the plan was to go into operation. So far everything had gone like clockwork, but now Jud had been told on Pickles' encrypted telephone that it was important to show the negotiator who was boss.

"You don't have to antagonize me, Kevin. I know this radio here is just for me to be able to hear you. I know you've put cameras and bugs in the wall. I know you can see everything that's going on in here, so I don't even need to take a hostage outside to kill them to show you I mean business, do I?"

"Let's slow things down, shall we?"

"No, Kevin, if you're not careful I will speed things up. Now I know that all you care about is Harwood, right? You don't care if we kill the lot of them, as long as your beloved Commander in Chief is okay. Am I right?"

Bo was clapping as he chewed on the last of the cold pizza,

his lips smacking as he chewed open mouthed. He clapped so hard he dropped his pistol from his hand, and it clattered to the floor. He was still giggling like a loon as he bent to pick it up, holding the crust of the pizza in his teeth like the finest Havana cigar.

"Let me kill one, Pa," Bo said looking at the hostages. "Let me kill an old one. No one will miss him."

The faces of the zip-locked together hostages twisted in horror, eyes pleading with Jud to keep his son away from them.

"Enough of this!" Harwood was on his feet and Pavlina was reaching a hand out to him.

"Martin, please, don't"

Harwood looked at his wife with a pained expression. "I can't just stand by and let him slaughter innocents. Are you listening, Kevin? This is President Harwood and this is a direct order from your Commander in Chief. You are not to accede to any of Elkins' demands. None of them. If it ends in my death, then so be it. I give you and your commanding officer full authority to storm the church and get this over with now. Let the devil take the hind most."

Jud threw his head back and laughed. "Shall I tell him, or will you, Kevin? I think the President is has been under a lot of stress at the moment and he's forgotten article three of the twenty-fifth amendment of the United States constitution, hasn't he?"

The radio remained silent other than the slight hiss of static as Jud released the mic button. He pressed it again. "Ok,

Kevin. I'll tell him."

Jud turned to Harwood , "And I quote, 'Whenever the President transmits to the President pro tempore of the Senate and the Speaker of the House of Representatives his written declaration that he is unable to discharge the powers and duties of his office, and until he transmits to them a written declaration to the contrary, such powers and duties shall be discharged by the Vice President as Acting President.' We've already had confirmation that Vice President Mulray is in charge now. You have been relieved of duties until you can resume them unhindered by our little party here."

Harwood's face pinked around the cheeks. "I am still President, Kevin! I give the orders. Take them all down now!"

Jud began to count. "Ten...nine...eight...seven...six... five...four...three... two...one... Nope. I don't think that they're going to be following your orders, Mister President. Not for a while yet. Now, Pickles. Put. Him. Down."

"With pleasure."

Pickles stepped forward and punched Harwood in the kidney. The President went down on one knee and gasped. The first lady began to sob and reached for his shoulder. Harwood pushed her hand away and thudded onto his backside on the altar.

Henri looked at the floor and the rest of the hostages were silent.

"So now we've dealt with that, Kevin, are you going to do what I say?"

"It's going to be difficult, but I'll see what I can do."

"You'll better than that," Jud spat into the mic. "If every one of your people are not pushed back at least one mile from the church I will start killing hostages. If after the next hour I can see any one of you within a mile of the church I will start killing hostages. And believe me I know. I have people where you least expect them, inside and outside this church. Follow my orders, Kevin, or people will die. Tick tock, Kevin. Tick tock."

* * * * *

Bullets clattered around Cody as he jumped, wind milling his arms through the air. The roof of the bank was beneath his feet and he hit the concrete, rolled and was up running again. The shouting had come, he thought from behind him, but the gunshots had come from his left side.

That didn't compute right now, but he didn't have time to think about it. He sprinted on, covering the roof at full tilt. The bank ended, and there was another fifteen-foot gap between it and the next building. But there was also a one story drop to contend with, as the next property on main street was not as tall and considerably thinner than the bank. It was however much longer and was part of a construction, perhaps a row of stores that had been built at the same time, which had then been carved up between different businesses.

"Follow him!" the shouts, from whoever they were, were still behind him but they were further away. In his prime, Cody could run the 100 yards in 11 seconds flat. He felt he wasn't far behind that record now as he sprinted on, even fifteen years older, and in cowboy boots.

Another shot tore into the roof ahead of him as he pelted forward. The chips it threw up clattered into his shins. That meant the shouting was coming from behind, but the shooting was now coming from in front. Whoever was shooting was high up and mobile.

Jack had another forty yards of building before he'd have to jump again, and there was a very good chance he was running towards a sniper.

Jack began to zig-zag in his trajectory across the roof. Using random strides to choose when to tack right or left. Standard operating procedure when you're exposed and under fire in a foreign war zone. Not a condition you expect to be in on an Arizona rooftop.

Two more bullets whistled by as he ran—both far enough away for Cody to know that he was employing the right tactic, and that the sniper was nothing like a trained sharpshooter. He was probably an interested amateur rather than a true professional—used to shooting deer or bear, not human prey.

Twenty yards to go, but with the haring left and right Cody would need to cover double that in strides before he got to the edge. He couldn't see a building up ahead, and he had no idea what the gap was going to be to the next rooftop, but Cody was too out in the open here to stop and take stock of what was to come.

It would have to be a blind leap of faith—if he stopped, the pursuers and the sniper would be on him in moments.

The edge of the store complex came up fast. He was at least thirty feet in the air and running at full speed. If there was no roof on beyond this one, however good he was at falling, and rolling he was going to break a ankle.

But a broken ankle was better than being shot he told himself, zagging after a zig and getting showered with more chips of concrete from the roof as he belted across is.

Ten more strides.

Five.

Another shot, this one so close it seared the top of his jacket and opened the material like an expert filleting a fish. But Cody had escaped injury—well at least until he knew what he was about to leap out into space onto.

There was no building to drop down onto on the other side of the store complex. There was a hard, concrete parking area and a loading bay for the supermarket at this end of town.

There may have been no building to arrest his thirty-foot drop, but there *were* two refrigerated trucks parked in the bay and Cody landed on the top of the nearest to his leaping off point.

He came down hard and only one of his feet had made it onto the top of the truck. He threw himself to the left, swinging his body away from the drop before he tumbled off the side of the truck and landed on his head on the concrete below.

The momentum he'd built up was drained away as he log-rolled across the roof of the truck, and in two seconds he found himself on the other side of it, rolling off that side.

"Gahhhhh!"

Jack grappled desperately to catch onto the side wall, or any point of purchase he could latch onto. His fingers just grabbed at empty air. All he could do was push his legs around as he fell so that he would land on his feet rather than his face.

Still travelling faster than was optimal, Cody dropped the last twelve feet to the ground, and yet again bent and rolled. Two bullets thumped into the side of the truck just inches from where his head had been before he'd dropped to the concrete.

Jack dived under the truck, rolled across the oily concrete and came out the other side. He began sprinting across the loading area.

He had no real idea where the sniper shots were coming from, other than a vague sense of their general direction but he was trying to keep the trucks in between him and where he *thought* they might be coming from.

The further he sprinted across the loading area the more aware he became that eventually the cold reality of geometry would expose his running figure to the sniper again.

But even with that idea in his head, Cody would not stop his feet from pounding, his body from zig-zagging, or his mind from thinking *who the hell is shooting at me?*

CHAPTER 22

It was only when the Range Rover Evoque went by her for the third time that Sara began to suspect she was being followed.

Sara had left the crowd by the hospital when she'd seen federal agents decamp from their vehicles and start scanning the crowd.

A number of terrorists, both domestic and foreign, had been known to enjoy rubbernecking the devastation they'd caused from the center of a crowd come to watch. Agents would be dispatched to walk the line at roadblocks to cast their eyes over the faces watching the emergency services at work. Sara herself, when she'd been training, had been sent out a number of times for this duty. It was essential work, but often thankless.

The agents who'd turned up, ordinarily would only be looking for known terrorists, their sympathizers or whack-job white supremacists with too much hate in their hearts and a surfeit of fertilizer to turn into bombs.

As soon as she'd seen the agents, Sara had turned on her heel and left the vicinity as inconspicuously as she could.

But now she knew that going to the hospital might have been a mistake of epic proportions. She hadn't been thinking straight, the shock of the explosion, and the need to get to the hospital to have her worst fears about the woman in the Subaru confirmed, and she was going to pay the price for that misstep.

She was walking briskly away from Navy Med south on Wisconsin Avenue, trying to work out where she could get to quickly enough to stay for the night. She'd need a place where she could pay in cash and not give ID. She couldn't risk turning up at any of her friend's apartments. There was a good chance those places would already be under surveillance.

Sara determined that her best shot might be to get across the Potomac River into Arlington. There she was sure she'd find a no-tell motel there where they'd take her paper money and not ask too many questions.

But the dark green Evoque told her that she might not even make it as far as the nearest bridge.

There were two dark figures in the vehicle. Their eyes were fixed ahead as the car drove past on the third go around. The last thing they were going to do was look at her, but there was a very good chance she'd already been IDed walking away from the hospital.

Facial recognition technology was coming into wider operation for law enforcement and intelligence services in the U.S. and around the world. If they'd already scanned the crowd from a vantage point Sara hadn't been aware of then it was also possible that she'd been made before she'd even seen the agents arrive.

It was thoroughly depressing to think that all the smart technologies she and her department relied on would now be ranged against her. She could only guess at how many people in the service had been compromised.

She'd left the Special Activities Center after the attack in the locker room without telling anyone where she was going and why she was going. At the time it felt exactly the right thing to do—the Center had been infiltrated, and if she'd stayed she might be dead already like the woman from the Subaru in the hospital explosion. But going out in the streets and not getting out of Washington could be just as dangerous.

Sara quickened her pace.

The Evoque didn't come back, she kept looking back along the line of traffic and forward for it, but it didn't show. That meant one of two things. Maybe she'd been mistaken, and the car didn't hold anyone coming to look for her, or they'd parked up somewhere, and were now following her on foot.

She paused at a Citibank ATM—not to take out any money—but to see if any dark shadows dipped back into cover back along Wisconsin Avenue. At this time of the night, there were very few people on the avenue anyway, and tailing someone under those conditions was going to be difficult—but not impossible.

If Sara had been running the operation to trail her, she'd have already put one of the agents ahead, as well as one behind—containing her. Looking the other way, south again in the direction of travel, there was no one ahead she could see, other than a young couple, worse the wear for drink, or high, walking hand in hand, crossing the road and laughing.

Sara started walking again, she was still four miles from the river and even then, she was still going to have to find somewhere to stay. There was a Double Tree just across the way, but they would want all sorts of assurance and identification, so it was pointless even thinking of trying there.

She carried on, head down, but scanning the sidewalk ahead and looking behind when she could.

As she reached a cross walk, a hand seemed to come out of nowhere and tap her on the shoulder.

"Sara...?"

The chain link fence on the perimeter of the loading bay was an easy enough barrier for Cody to scale under normal circumstances. Knowing that he would now be fully exposed to the sniper and moving slowly enough to be picked off by even the most amateur of snipers, didn't make the climb any less appetizing but he had to monkey himself up the fence and flip himself over the top.

Under any normal circumstances in an urban warfare setting like this Cody would have gone to cover, found a place of refuge to catch his breath and make a plan.

But he didn't have time for that. He'd made it past the National Guard and away from whoever was tracking him, but he was still half a mile from Hacker and getting news to him about Brant's mercenaries and their planned rescue attempt on the church.

He dived for the fence and dug his fingers between the links, digging the pointed toes of his boots in hard as the metal took his weight with just a suggestion of bowing out.

A shot stung the aluminum by his hand and he flinched but kept swarming upwards. He kicked a foot over, and flung the rest of his body after it, rolling over the top of the fence and dropping hard over the other side into an area of landscaped Bee Brush behind a concrete curb. It cushioned his fall a little, but the thud of hitting the ground still took the wind out of him. Another sniper shot pinged into the fence, but it was six or seven feet above him. Whoever was doing the shooting as just hitting and hoping now.

Jack was back on the utility access road behind the stores, which had been road blocked by the National Guard five hundred yards back. Here the road was tree lined and there were fences backing onto the business, but ahead the fences ran out, and there was a patch of open ground across a vacant lot.

Jack jogged rather than sprinted across the lot, wary that he was a little more exposed, but secure in the knowledge there were a few more buildings now between him and wherever the sniper had been on the other side of main street.

His thinking processes could kick back in now the headlong rush to escape had dropped to a comfortable jog and he tried to get his head around who might have been doing the shooting.

All of Brant and his men had left Dry Mouth PD—the chances it wasn't any of them, because, a) they were on the mission to raid the church and more importantly, b) they didn't seem like the kind of guys who would miss Cody, however had he zig-zagged. There's no way anyone with Kellerman and Mike could have made it to a vantage point—with a sniper rifle and he certainly hadn't seen one in the Police Department offices—sure some of them may have followed him out into the night and seen that he was climbing up the fire escape, but he'd left them behind with their desperate shouting pretty easily as he'd hared across the rooftops.

So that left the uncomfortable thought, that a sniper had positioned himself, high on a rooftop in the center of town for another reason than taking pot shots at Cody. That high up he would have a clear view of the church and what was happening around it.

If he was an agent sharpshooter, then like Brant's men he wouldn't have missed Cody as he'd run over the rooftops.

So, he was either a whacko getting ready to make a name for himself—unlikely—why hadn't he started shooting earlier? Why had he shot just at Cody and no one else?

So, if not a killer-for-kicks. Then who?

The really uncomfortable conclusion was that the sniper, whoever he was, was in some way connected to Elkins and the people in the church.

Another piece of critical information to pass on to Hacker if he ever got to him.

Now across the lot and still jogging, Cody heard a rumble of traffic from main street. Such was the oddness of the sound. Hearing so much engine noise and movement this time of night, in the relatively quiet town gave him pause. The echoing from the entrance of a short alley between a pawn broker, and a convenience store stopped Cody's forward progress in its tracks.

Jack looked along the twenty-yard alley and was more than surprised to see a line of military vehicles grumbling by, casting flickering shadows down the walls on either side. There were National Guardsmen too, walking along main street, and then most surprising of all, plain wrapper SUVs and the Secret Service Command Truck, where Cody had met Hacker all those hours ago, rolled by too.

All of it, every soldier, every federal agent, every vehicle and every truck were running along main street, *away* from the church where the president was being held hostage.

CHAPTER 23

"Sara...? Sara Durell?"

Sara flinched as the hand brushed her and then fell away. She spun, making fists, ready to punch, kick, fight—to do anything she had to get away.

She didn't recognize the man in the grey suit. He was in his mid-thirties. Black regulation military short, his chin looked cut from granite. Under the streetlight his eyes were hooded, but his mouth was in a smile.

"Oh, this is really embarrassing. You don't remember me, do you?"

Sara blinked. No, she didn't. "I..."

"I almost didn't recognize you myself under the baseball hat. Didn't know you were a Redskins fan."

The man walked into the spray of light from a neon sign, and Sara got to look in his eyes. A vague recollection was shouldering its way up through her mind, which then blossomed into a memory.

"Roger...Roger Lloyd?"

Roger smiled. "Got it in one. I was worried there I'd become one of those guys who didn't touch the sides."

"You were on attachment from Crime Sciences to the Special Services center. You came to my Terrorist Ideology Theory lecture. Asked some tough questions."

"I can see why you'd want to forget me then!"

Roger looked at his watch. "So, what are you doing out here at one AM in the morning walking along Wisconsin avenue? I know why I am. I went to see if there was anything I could do to help at the explosion. But they looked like they had it all covered, and Crime Science won't be sticking their noses into it until tomorrow I guess when the sun comes up. You were doing the same I guess?"

Sara nodded. "Yeah. So wired, I thought I'd walk back to the office. There's no way I'm getting any sleep tonight."

"Same here. Terrible business. What with the President an' all. Really feels like we're under attack again in our own backyard. Didn't think I'd be feeling like that again after the twin towers."

Sara looked at her watch, and realized that it wasn't on her wrist, and so continued moving the hand up to her baseball cap and adjusted the brim. "Look, Roger, I'm really not very good company right now, I want to get back to the office. I really should call a cab."

Roger grinned. "Oh, that's okay. Your ride's here now."

The green Evoque slid to a halt alongside them, and the punch Roger delivered to Sara's gut pushed ever atom of breath from her lungs and sent her crashing to the sidewalk.

* * * * *

"They're doing it! They're doing it!"

Bo was almost jumping with delight. He was using a pair of the SWAT teams' field glasses to look through the window of the vestibule as the surrounding ring of federal agents, marines and Secret Service men withdrawing to Jud's stipulated distance of one mile.

The hostages' faces were grim with fear. The first lady had her head in her hands, and the President's face was a stony mask of hatred.

Bo ran from the front of the church laughing and whooping, stopping by the President and tickling him under the chin. "You ain't in charge no more, your worship. My daddy is the President of the United States now."

Harwood moved his head back, and Bo made a fist, ready to strike. Jud caught his hand as it swung down. "No, son, not yet. You'll get your fun, but you have to be patient."

"But I don't want to be patient, Daddy. I want to just mush his face a little. I promise I won't break anything."

Jud shook his head and pulled Bo away from the orbit of the President. He put his mouth close to his son's ear. "If we hurt him, they're not going to do the things we want. They'll calculate that we're going to kill everyone anyway whatever demands they agreed to and they'll just come in. We need to get to at least to eight AM. Fourteen eighty-eight. Remember that son. This is bigger than all of us. When I make that statement, at the correct time the world will change. Don't do anything to mess that up before it happens. Okay?"

Bo looked at his shoes. "Ok, Daddy. I promise. But he sure has a hittable face."

"He's a politician, son. That's what all their faces look like to me, too."

Bo grinned and almost skipped to the window to look again at the withdrawing authorities.

"We need to speak about the welfare of the hostages."

Jud turned to hear the voice of the curate—David Cody, he'd said his name was—coming across the church. His voice was calm, and it was strong. It didn't match the expressions on the faces of the hostages. The first lady took her head from her hands to watch. The President's expression softened.

"I said we need to talk about the welfare of the hostages," David said again, this time adding "If we can, Mister Elkins."

Jud set his chin imperiously, "*You're* one of the hostages, Cody. I'm guessing that like all you religious folks the only welfare you're concerned with is your own and our dollars pouring into your tax free bank accounts."

David shook his head. "I am neither an evangelical, or after money. This is a community church that serves the people of Dry Mouth to the best of our ability. There's a donations box on the way out but that's it. We don't appear in revival tents, we don't holler on TV, and we don't have tax free bank accounts."

"Thank you for the CV. But why are you polluting my ears right now?"

"I'm concerned. If we don't let people start to use the facilities at the back of the church soon the conditions are going to become intolerable. I'm sure you don't want that. Secondly, other than a few sodas and a slice of pizza no one here has eaten or drunk anything for over twelve hours. There will be people who need to take their medication. There are others who might need their injections. I'm not trying to trick you, Mister Elkins—like maybe you thought Kevin the negotiator was—I am genuinely concerned for the people here as they are here and now. I'm not asking you to release anyone, but I am asking you to show some compassion to them."

Jud grunted. "That's a mighty long speech for a man short on time, son."

"I've been thinking. You could station a man or two in near the bathroom. There are no windows in there, so no one will be able to escape. You could send people in there one at a time to attend to their physical needs. Reverend Just and I could go to our kitchen and bring out water and cups. We could even make tea or coffee. You have enough men to make sure we don't get up to anything you wouldn't approve of—we give you our word that we will not try anything. We just want to make sure everyone gets what they need."

Jud began walking over towards the curate. He was a strong looking boy. Handsome some might say. The thing about him that upset Jud so much was that he was not at all scared. Even Reverend Just, sitting on the floor next to the curate had a face that could spook a herd at nine hundred paces, but the younger man had an effortless grace about him that in another time, Jud may have found beguiling.

"You not scared of me, boy?"

"I'm terrified, Mister Elkins. I've never been this close to death before. I'm not scared of dying, no, I'm scared of the pain and the agony I might go through getting there. But I do know that if I do die, that it will be because of God's plan, not yours. It will be his decision. Not yours, and Mister Elkins, in that case I've got nothing to lose by asking you to let these poor people use the bathroom and have to let them drink some water. How about it?"

"How about you let me mush the priest's face a little, Daddy? Might shut him up."

Jud shook his head, "Do you know what, Bo? I don't think it would."

He took a step back from David and considered the full length of the body.

"If I'm going to shut you up, then I'm going to hafta shoot you, son."

"If that's what God wills, then so be it."

There was a gasp from the hostages as Jud raised his pistol and cocked it. Pavlina Harwood got to her feet, hands on the side of her head, "No! No! Stop this madness! Leave him alone!"

The President was getting to his feet, but Pickles put a hand on his shoulder and forced him back down on the altar.

Jud held the pistol steady. The sights on David's forehead, just above his eyes.

"I don't believe in God," Jud said.

CHAPTER 24

Hands were reaching down to Sara on the sidewalk. She was winded but she was not disabled. As the fog cleared from her head and she put her sheer stupidity aside at being duped by Roger Lloyd, she grabbed the pinky finger on the hand digging into her collar and broke it.

In a fight, you don't have to always go for the haymaker—you can get just as much advantage with sharp, agonizing non-critical injury pain as you could from a punch, a kick or a head-butt.

It was always about fighting smarter, not fighting harder.

The hand came away, but his other hand formed, as Sara had predicted, a sledgehammer fist which was going to be used immediately to retaliate for the broken finger. As the fist whistled down, Sara tuned her body sideways, and it crunched into the concrete of the sidewalk. The guy who had been above her squawked like a chicken having its neck wrung and fell away backwards.

Roger, who was holding onto her ankles because before

she'd started fighting back, the plan was obviously for Roger to take one end and Pinky to take the other before they bundled her into the Range Rover.

Sara tried twisting her feet out from his grip, but it was iron.

"Settle down, bitch. It's not our orders to kill you but, right now I'm not about following orders."

Sara twisted again, reached inside the overcoat and pulled out the Glock.

"Jesus, she's got a gun. No one said anything about a gun," shouted Pinky.

This was going real well for them.

Roger was fumbling inside his jacket where the butt of a pistol could clearly be seen in a holster flapping about behind the material.

Sara fired behind her to where Pinky's voice had been coming from.

The squawk became a scream and a body went down yelling, "My leg! My leg!" as it thudded against the side of the Evoque and crashed to the sidewalk.

Roger had his hand on the pistol inside his jacket and was beginning to draw it out. Sara levelled the Glock on his heart. "I'm not likely to miss from here, now am I?"

Roger's hand froze and he put his hand up. Lights were coming on in the widows above the stores. Perhaps a 911 call had already gone in. If Roger and Pinky had legit ID and the cops showed up mob handed, she was probably not going to be able to talk her way out of this.

Sara covered Roger and got up.

Pinky's hands were dark with blood. The bullet had hit him in the leg just below his right kneecap. His fingers, even the broken one, were slithering in the blood over the wound. He was a short thin man with curly hair and a mustache that might have time-warped from the 80s.

"Give me your gun, Roger. Now, or I'll be putting bullets in your leg too. I don't have to kill you, but as I'm sure your friend here will tell you, there are some pains worse than death."

Roger nodded, pulled out a SIG with his fingertips, and passed it to Sara. She put it in her belt. Reaching down to Pinky, but keeping the gun on Roger, she took a second SIG from the holster beneath his jacket.

"Get him in the car." Sara said to Roger, looking up and down Wisconsin Avenue to see if the Range Rover had back up, of if the police were starting to take an interest.

"I need to be taken to the hospital. I didn't sign up for this, Roger. I didn't sign up for anything like this! I'm politics! I'm not spy stuff!"

"Shut your stupid mouth before I kill you myself, Sullivan."

Sullivan's mouth clamped shut but his fingers still dug into the material of his pants. Roger stepped forward, put his hands underneath the shot man's arms and hauled him up. Sullivan sagged, his face sheened with sweat, and Roger had to grunt to get him on to the back seat of the Evoque.

Sullivan slithered across the leather.

Sara, keeping the gun on Roger, got onto the seat next to Sullivan. "Roger. Get in from the passenger side and move across. You're driving."

Roger did as he was told. She racked the SIG and used it to cover Sullivan, while her Glock was on the side of Roger's head.

"Drive."

"Where to?"

"Where you were supposed to take me."

Roger put the car into drive and pulled away from the sidewalk.

Sara dug the SIG into Sullivan's side. "Where were you supposed to be taking me?"

"I don't know." Sullivan replied. Even though he was bleeding and injured, Sara knew a lie when she heard it. "Sullivan. Really. Do I have to shoot you again? They didn't even tell you that I might be armed before sending you out to get shot. I don't think you owe them any loyalty now, do we?"

Sullivan's mouth clamped shut. Even the whimpering about his wound had ceased. He screwed up his eyes expecting to be shot.

Damn.

Sara realized that defending the location of who had sent Roger and Sullivan to take her was preferable to dying.

✳ ✳ ✳ ✳ ✳

"Yow sure about this, Brant? I mean really sure?" Vick whispered to the actor.

Vick was laying in the scrub two hundred yards from the

rear of the church. Brant lay beside him, smearing black camouflage paint on his cheeks. He was a little out of breath from the hike away from the Humvee and was glad of the chance to rest, but his heart was hammering as much from excitement as it was from exertion.

His thoughts bubbled brightly with what was to come—how he would be seen and what the press would write about the acting action hero, who'd put his ass where his mouth was.

Segal might have been a cop before he went crazy, and Clint had been a successful politician as his public service, and even Regan had become President. But how many of them had saved a President from terrorists. The money, respect and power were going to roll over him in a tide. He would be pooping cash for a thousand movies after today.

"Of course, I'm sure, Vick. You've showed me enough times how to fire one of these suckers."

Brant held up the MP5 against his tactical vest. He'd changed into combat blacks, pants and boots as they'd moved the Humvee off the road, without headlights, guided by Sharon driving in NVD goggles. Brant and the others had been more than surprised to see the forces who had been in a ring around the church, pulling back down the road away from it. Through binoculars, Vick had looked towards the church lit up by arc lights, and the sagging rotored *Marine One* Sea King next to it and breathed. "What the hell? Yon soldiers and agents. They're all moving back. Why?"

"No idea," Sharon had replied. "Demands from the terrorists, I s'pose, guv."

Vick looked hard at Brant. "Yow stay at the back. Yow keep behind me. I'll keep you alive, but if I tell yow to get the hell out of there yow better do as I tells yow. We clear on that, bab?"

"Yes. As crystal. It's just a bunch of hillbillies who go lucky. We...I mean you guys can take them out right?"

"It's not just hillbillies in there," Sharon said, her face already near invisible in the dark after the application of the paint. "There's at least three SWAT and two Secret Service agents. We don't know if they've secreted more of their people in with the hostages. And why haven't they made any demands yet? They must be supremely confident not to be pushing things along and being happy to wait. I still reckon we can do this, but don't be surprised if, like, there are more surprises."

Brant shook his head. "Guys, you know I need this. You know why. If we pull this off, we'll be covered in gravy until doomsday. I know I'm asking a lot, but if your guys are as good as you say they are..."

"They are," Vick and Sharon said in unison.

"Then," Brant continued, "within the hour we're going to be heroes."

"I'm not saying we're not going to be heroes, bab, but I'm just worried about taking you in there."

"Don't be," said Brant. "Just concentrate on the mission. Oscars for everyone, Vick. Oscars for everyone."

Vick nodded, but his eyes were still not sure. "Boxer?"

One of the mercenaries, a huge American large enough to

land F-15s across his back came forward on his elbows. Eyes white in the black face paint. "Boss?"

His voice was a low as a rattlesnake's belly and filled with more southern gravel that the shores of the Mississippi.

"Brant is yours. Do not let him out of arm's length for a bloody second. Keep him behind the bullets and at the first sign of us being compromised in any way, yow drag him out of there back to the Humvee. I don't mind if yow have do it by his bloody balls. If he gives yow any trouble yow have permission to deck him and take him out stat. Understood?"

Boxer saluted and smiled at Brant. "You're my bitch now."

Brant smiled, but inside he was losing a little of his confidence. It was draining out of his belly, and his legs felt a little like they were walking away from him on their own. Vick's words had chimed more than he had expected them to. He looked towards the church. Clapboard walls blasted by the arc lights—like a UFO had landed among the scrub. In fact, it was lit up like a film set, but this wasn't a film.

A film set would have stunt doubles, blank rounds and a director to call cut if things went awry—there was none of that to help him now—but he couldn't go back.

He needed this. He needed it bad.

Vick, Sharon and Boxer would keep him alive. Or they would die trying.

CHAPTER 25

Jack skidded to a stop at the bottom of the alley. Everyone but everyone was pulling back. If he'd stayed at the other end of town, the Hacker and the Command Truck would have come to him. The irony of the situation was not lost on him. As he squinted a look around the corner. The last of the National Guard Tahoe's worked their way along main street, their taillights winking and reflecting off windows.

This had not been a partial withdrawal from around the church; this was a complete retreat. Either the Elkins had decreed it, or the government were getting ready for a surgical airstrike on the church, and as Cody guessed the President was still in there, he didn't think that was the likeliest of notions.

He thumped his fist into the wall. Following the command truck back into town was likely to expose him to the sniper, Kellerman, Mike and anyone else who was being sent out to find him.

He didn't know how far back into town they were going, so he didn't know how long—and even if he'd be able to for that matter—it would be before he could get through to Hacker.

If he closed his eyes now, Cody was sure he would see a Technicolor picture of the sands of time running inexorably out. The options were narrowing by the second.

Jack was going to have to stop Brant and the others himself. And right now, he was going to have to do it without any weapons or equipment.

Dammit, how he'd wished he'd been able to stop for a gun as he'd hared from Dry Mouth PD.

No time to stop and think about what you regret now, Jack. Time to act if you're going to stop a massacre of epic proportions.

Jack ducked back down the alley and jogged out the other side. He headed down the access road behind the stores again in the direction of the church. He was sheltered by long messy ranks of yellow paloverde which lined this part of the road.

In fifty or so yards he was away from the commercial part of Dry Mouth, and into the bungalows and ranch style houses of a small residential district.

From what he remembered of his previous trips to Dry Mouth, back when he and Kelly had their brief thing, there were only twenty or thirty houses here. Go beyond them and one would reach the scrubby brush on the outskirts of town. From there you'd get into the wide lot on which the church—isolated and alone—stood. The church was like a last defiant gasp of Dry Mouth's place in the landscape, before the road

turned south west to join Arizona route 82 towards Nogales
and the border with Mexico.

It was rough, near desert country, and the church stood
like the gatepost to it. He could see it now between the roofs
of these evacuated houses—blasted white by the Federal
agent's spotlights.

Pointing up like a middle finger to the desert.

Then a thought struck him.

If the houses around him had been evacuated here, and
since then, the National Guard and the federal circus had
rumbled itself out of the picture. There was going to be a least
a couple of houses here worth breaking into if he was going to
take it to Brant and the others.

Jack knelt in the road and clicked out the compartment
from his boot heel.

* * * * *

Sullivan hadn't opened his eyes, and Sara hadn't shot him
again.

Yet.

She'd made Roger point the Evoque off Wisconsin Avenue
and head east into Chevy Chase, with its large well-appointed
houses, but well away from, yet parallel to, the government
districts around Pennsylvania Avenue, the White House and
the Special Activities Center.

In a parking lot behind an elementary school and a wide-
open municipal park they'd parked the car, and with Sullivan

still on the back seat, she'd made Roger get out of the Evoque, and open the tailgate at gun point.

"You can run, but you won't be able to hide, Sara. This is bigger than all of us. Me, you—the President."

"Just open it."

Roger did as he was told.

Inside the plush, well upholstered interior were a number of silver flight cases. The kind you might see being loaded onto the back of a truck by roadies after a gig—they were perhaps the size of an electric guitar but three times as deep and were padlocked closed.

"Do I have to frisk you to find a key to open them up?"

Roger shook his head and gingerly reached inside his pants pocket and pulled out a keyring, which jangled dully.

He opened the first flight case and turned it so Sara could see what was inside. It was packed with equipment. CS gas canisters, gas masks, handcuffs, night sticks, body armor, night vision goggles and stacks of magazines for submachine guns.

The second flight case was opened to reveal the Mp5s to go with the magazines, two grenade launchers, and packed into a foam cube like eggs in a carton, were two dozen high explosive grenades to compliment the launchers. As the flight cases had been moved aside, she could see in the depths of the Evoque, against the back seat were stacked piles of tactical helmets. Each with the word PLEDGE stenciled on the surface in silver cargo font.

"Going to a war?"

"Going to start one, yeah." Roger said matter-of-factly. "So, like I said, Sara. This is bigger than you could ever know."

"I could turn you in. Make you drive to the nearest police station and show them what's in the trunk."

"Be my guest, Sara. This stuff is my third drop in Washington and Maryland in the last three days. The week before we were in Michigan. The week before that Illinois. And we're not the only ones making deliveries like this. It's happening all over the country. And at eight o'clock tomorrow morning you'll find out exactly what we're going to achieve."

"Why at eight AM?"

Roger's eyes widened with surprise. "And you a top- notch intelligence operative, well regarded, and smart as a silver button. You can't work it out?"

Eight a.m.

August is the 8th Month.

And *goddammit* if now they were after midnight and August 13th and flipped over to August 14th. A cold dread dripped into her heart.

"Fourteen eighty-eight—the fourteen words." she said as the realization hit. "*We must secure the existence of our people and a future for white children,* followed by *Heil Hitler* – H being the 8th letter of the alphabet."

"You got it, sister. Top of the class."

This was no longer a movement of spotty inadequate Incels and potbellied redneck racists waving their Tiki-torches in Charlottesville, chanting, *"Jews will not replace us,"* because it gave the sorry sacks of shit a hard on. Now they were being armed—properly armed. And that heinous process was linked with the President being taken hostage in Dry Mouth.

What better way to start a revolution than take down the commander in chief, thus prove that the government is ineffectual because it could not save him, and that the United States' national symbol of continuity could be destroyed so easily.

Sara was reeling at the thought, but kept the gun trained on Roger, even though she wanted to throw it down, crawl under the car and die, right here, right then.

But then the coldness of shock in her froze her insides into hard resolve. She knew what she had to do.

"Close it up," she ordered, but not before she'd pulled two pairs of handcuffs from the first flight case. "I don't care how scared Sullivan or you are about telling me where you were going to take me, but you're going to tell me where it is one way or another."

The park was still quiet, the elementary school dark, the nearest houses were a good three hundred yards away through the beech trees and oaks still in full leaf. They weren't going to be disturbed.

Sara handcuffed Roger to the steering wheel and after pocketing the key fob starter, told him, "I will shoot you if you say anything, anything at all, is that clear?"

Roger didn't nod, but she could see in his eyes that he understood perfectly.

Sara opened the rear door and pulled Sullivan out into the dirt. He crashed down with a sob. He'd lost a considerable amount of blood and was pale around the gills. She handcuffed him to the inner face of the Evoque's door and hunkered down next to him.

"They didn't tell you that I might have a gun. They didn't tell you I fight like a hell cat. What did they tell you about me?"

"The woman in the Subaru. Was that your handy work?"

Sullivan shook his head. His eyes flicked to the driver's seat.

"Roger like beating up on women, does he?"

She heard a snort of derision from the front of the car. Whoever had beaten up the woman they had enjoyed it. No one does that much damage when a bullet in the head will give the cleanest and quickest result. Roger had wanted her to suffer.

"What was her name?" Sara said. "Tell me who she was."

And so he told her.

Oh, mother of God.

The name did more than ring a bell. It unlocked half of the darkness around this whole thing. The name was unusual enough to be memorable to say the least, not at all common. In fact, she'd only heard the name once before, and it belonged to...

"Okay, my kneecapped friend, it's like this. They didn't tell you all that stuff about me, what do you think I do for the CIA?"

"I don't know. They just said you were in intelligence, and we needed to bring you in to find out what you knew and who you've told."

"A sensible plan. Now, going back to my particular skill set, what do you know about extraordinary rendition?"

"I don't."

"Extraordinary rendition is the name given to the practice of taking enemy terrorist combatants from their combat zone, to a third country rather than bringing them back to the United States first. Do you know why?"

"No."

"Because torture, under the Geneva Convention is illegal."

"So?"

"So we don't want to carry out torture on United States soil, but some people have so much useful information they're not willing to give freely, that occasionally, they have to be deposited in a country where the Geneva Convention isn't number one on the priorities list."

Sullivan looked up. His glassy eyes suddenly full of concern. "You going to take me out of the United States...to be tortured...that's...illegal."

Sara almost snorted but carried on. "No, I'm not going to send you out of the country. You see when those enemy combatants, or as we like to call them terrorists, reach that designated country outside the auspices of the Geneva Convention, do you know who's waiting for them?"

Sullivan shook his head.

"Me," said Sara reaching down to undo the buttons of Sullivan's blood-stained shirt. "So, shall we get started?"

CHAPTER 26

Jud had never taken kindly to his authority being challenged, and Pickles was getting close to the line. Ever since Jud had dropped his gun barrel, and agreed to let the mouthy curate David Cody arrange for the hostages to use the bathroom in relays, watched over by the SWAT team rather than shot his face off, he'd noticed a change in the Secret Service agent. Water and candy bars—from the children's Sunday school—had been passed out among the captives and that had coincided with Pickles becoming somewhat of a thorn in his side.

Jud had not known Pickles or Blint before his organization had been contacted by those in Washington ready to help them take their cause to the next level. These shadowy benefactors had provided the intelligence, resources and had kept Jud's family hidden from the authorities since the raid on his home. The raid when Honeychild had been captured and the rest of the family had gone on the run.

There had been a series of safe houses they had been moved

through, while they had prepared for the taking of President Harwood. The weapons, the explosives and detonators had been provided at the last safe house, and the address of Henri Charon had been furnished. It had been a smooth operation, and Jud had been more than pleased to be part of it, adding what he saw as his own unique touches to it.

He'd been told to contact Pickles over the encrypted line, and Pickles had explained what he and Blint would be able to do, and that the organization had infiltrated the government at all local and national levels, that they had been waiting for this opportunity to come along for many years and Jud Elkins was just the man to carry it out. He had the knowledge, the verve and above all the commitment to the cause necessary. They had been watching his progress for many years and were pleased with him. Pickles had told Jud that he and Blint would be at his disposal, and they would work to his line.

But that was then, and this was now and ever since Jud had told Sandra what he was about to do, and Pickles had been on the periphery of the conversation, the Secret Service agent had been typing on his cell phone, and been reading the messages back and then typing furiously some more. And he hadn't been showing Jud the messages.

That wasn't part of the deal.

"What's up, boy?"

Jud had pulled Pickles away from the president and signaled to Sandra to go over and replace him. He'd walked the Secret Service agent to the entrance vestibule and now made it clear that he wasn't happy.

"For the last twenty minutes you've been on that thing," he pointed at the encrypted telephone. "Tippity-tapping away, reporting to the great and good—but you ain't been passing their messages on to me. Why?"

"All in good time Jud. But I have to tell you they're not happy. They are worried about your ideological purity when it comes to this mission."

"Ideological purity? What the hell are you talking about, boy?"

"You told Sandra you were going to speak to Kevin and demand the authorities bring Honeychild to the church."

"She's my daughter, and she's in jail. I want her out of there."

"That wasn't part of the deal."

"It's part of my deal."

"No, Jud. No. This has to been seen as a selfless act. When you make the statement at eight AM, it has to be seen as a call to arms. Any petty selfless concerns about your family, or your child, have to be put to one side."

Jud poked Pickles in the chest. "I ain't putting my daughter to one side boy, ya hear me, I ain't doing that for no one. At three AM, I'm gonna wake Kevin up, and I'm going to get my daughter here. And I don't care what you or our paymasters think of that."

"Your children have already compromised the mission, Elkins..."

"Oh, it's Elkins now is it, lost your friendly approach, have you? And I've killed men for lesser crimes than shit-talking my children. You take that back, son."

Pickles hissed, "We're entering the critical phase now. You know it, I know it. And we've got Bo acting like a cross between Rambo with his brains kicked out and a damn clown. Tod has disappeared off the grid and you want to delay things by making the authorities bring your psychotic daughter to the church. There can be no delay, Jud. There's a timetable here."

"I know all about your timetable and your darn fourteen eighty-eight, Pickles. I know all about your ideological purity and your Nazi propaganda. You can be proud of your whiteness, and that's fine. I am too. But I'm proud of my daughter more."

"They're going to get you out of the country, they're going to make sure you're safe. Your daughter can be brought to you later. They have the power and the influence to do that."

Jud shook his head. "Son, they're politicos. Sure, they may want to change things, sure they might have their powers and their influences, but let me tell you what I am. I have a love for my daughter that goes beyond any of your ideology. The people you work for wanted me for this thing because of my ideals and my desires for the country. They saw in me the right kind of American to make this work, and I am willing to be the scalpel that cuts the cancer from the heart of your nation, but I am going to want something in return, and that's going to be my daughter out of that prison, and back here in the bosom of my family. I will not settle for anything less. I hope you understand that, my Secret Service traitor."

The agent bristled at the word. "I am no traitor. I'm a patriot. Just like you."

"You're not like me, son. You're not like me at all. And there's just one reason for that."

"Oh yeah?"

"Yeah. You ain't no father to Honeychild Elkins. And if you was, boy, then you would understand."

"This is a crock…"

"I don't care what you think. I don't care what you tippi-ty-tap back to our paymasters in Washington."

"You will…"

"I will not. Now you will stand down, Pickles, and do as you're told. I'm getting my daughter here, and that's an end to it."

Jud cut any reply from Pickles dead with a single hand gesture and walked back into the body of the church. Bo, who was sitting on McDainel's coffin, kicking his legs like a toddler on the edge of a creek dangling his feet in the water.

"Everything okay, Dad?" he asked.

Jud said nothing, just stalked over to him, cuffed him around the head and pulled him off the coffin. "Behave yourself, show some respect and act like a damn professional, boy. This isn't a playground."

Jud sent a glance back to Pickles as if to say *satisfied?*

Pickles was walking out of the vestibule, straightening his tie. He nodded.

Jud pulled the radio from him pocket and hit the call button. "Wakey wakey, Kevin. I need to talk to your boss."

* * * * *

It wasn't until Cody had broken himself into the third house that he found what he'd been looking for, He'd wasted precious minutes in the first two properties, but here in the third he'd hit pay dirt.

The Brattonsound Sentinel Gun Safe was solid, impregnable to most non-subtle or unskilled attempts to open it.

But the seven-lever lock was only a little stubborn when it came to Cody's attempts to get it to give up its secrets.

Inside he found a Kel-Tec KSG, Pump Action, 12 Gauge, 12 Round shotgun which looked black as hell and twice as mean. The bullpup design—with action and magazine behind the trigger—gave the gun a compact size, without losing muzzle accuracy.

Jack had fired one before and felt comfortable with it. There were also enough shells for the owner to spend a good day skeet shooting. He found an ammo bag stuffed in a cupboard next to the gun safe, and so he filled it with shells.

Next to the KSG was a vintage Colt Cobra Diamondback with a four-inch barrel and clutch of speed loaders for fast re-priming. Cody put those in the ammo bag as well as two boxes of .38 shells. The Diamondback itself he loaded and put into the belt in the small of his back.

Before he left the property, his hand hovered over the landline—should he call Sara? Should he call anyone to warn them about what was about to go down. It was tempting for sure, but in the game of mirrors and shadows that was playing out above and below the surface of the hostile action in the church—who could he trust? He was sure that he could trust Sara, but who might she tell that they couldn't? Someone who might warn those in the church, or anyone that he was here in the hot zone trying to do what was right?

He snatched his hand away from the telephone and clenched his fist.

There was only one way through this right now and that was alone.

Jack kept his head low and ran in a crouch between the houses, and now had his clearest view yet of the church. The arc lights were going to give him one advantage, and that was he was going to be able to see when any of Brant's pay soldiers were getting ready to make their move. He knew they were well trained, and highly armed, but he was confident enough in his abilities to at least deflect them from their crazy mission.

The church blazed against the deep blue of the desert night. The catering tent was still in place, the tables still laden with food which had been left where it had been placed. Insects buzzed around it; fluttering motes in the light reflected from the church. *Marine One* was well illuminated too—it still looked too big and too incongruous for the location. Like it was an alien craft that had crash-landed from space on the ancient desert next to the church.

The area was eerily quiet but still felt oppressive and full of foreboding. Cody knew that what was going on inside the church would be anything other than matching silence or stillness outside it. It was as if waves of enmity from within were coming out, rippling over the landscape like radio waves.

From what he'd overheard of the planning for Brant's scheme before he'd been locked up, was the mercenaries were going to approach the church from the west, across the desert scrub but well away from the town. They couldn't have predicted, like Cody, that they were going to be given a free run with the government forces withdrawing into the town.

Jack looked at his watch. It was coming up to 3am. Any time in the next hour would be the prime time for the rescue attempt to commence. This was the golden time for missions of this nature—the hostages and the perpetrators would be at their most tired and edgy. Their reflexes dulled by exhaustion and prolonged tensions.

That Brant's forces hadn't begun their attack yet was a sign that they were waiting for what they thought was the optimum time to begin. Cody imagined them, out beyond the church, laying in the scrub, waiting for the go signal from Vick. If he'd been leading the mission, Cody would have sent one, perhaps two of his crew up to the rear of the church to see if they could get some intel on where the bad guys were, what the exposure might be like for finding the quickest entry into the building. But if Cody was leading the assault, there was one thing he wouldn't be doing right now—and that would be coming in from the ground.

Elkins and his cohorts were fully trained professionals. They would know that this was the optimal time for an assault. The men from the SWAT team, and the two Secret

Service turncoats would be alert and ready. They would have briefed the others, they would have kept themselves rested, so that their senses weren't dulled, or their bodies slowed and silted up with tiredness.

They weren't just going up against a bunch of amateurs here. There was a real chance of serious and sustained resistance.

Inside the church they would be ready for Brant, and Jack knew that.

After checking one last time his newly-acquired guns were ready to fire, he hefted the KSG in his hand and put the ammo bag over his shoulder.

Jack began his run, in a wide route outside the spray of reflected light. A route that would bring him around eventually to the western approach to the church.

With the only sound his feet moving swiftly over the rough ground, Jack moved low and fast, into the dark.

CHAPTER 27

Sara hadn't needed to touch Sullivan at all. He'd caved at the very suggestion of torture. She didn't have it in her heart to tell him that she'd never tortured anyone, was against it as a means to gathering intelligence—people who are tortured usually just tell you want they think you want to hear and will agree with anything to make it stop—but she wanted to keep the threat there in the background in case she needed more information out of Sullivan.

Roger had done as he'd been told, and kept silent in the driver's seat, but she could see the muscles working in his cheeks. He was grinding his teeth, and he was gripping the steering wheel so tight his knuckles were white as lasers.

Sara had helped Sullivan back into the Evoque and used a medikit from the back of the vehicle to perform some rudimentary first aid to the gunshot in his leg as a reward for the information. The wound was ragged and surrounded by congealing blood, which had now almost stepped seeping out. She could see jagged bone in the center of it, and Sullivan would need surgery to repair it, but there wasn't time for that now, and besides, she still needed him. Roger didn't look like he was going to be any more forthcoming for the moment.

When the wound was dressed, she'd given Sullivan some painkillers which he had gratefully swallowed dry. It was just after five in the a.m. and the city was starting to wake up. They needed to be on the road soon if they were going to get across the Potomac and drive south into McClean.

It was an area she knew by reputation only. A rich, upmarket neighborhood patronized by the great and good of Washington. Many politicos lived there. She knew Dick Cheney and Newt Gingrich were residents—or at least had been the last time the subject of who lives where had come up in the office tittle-tattle. McClean was stuffed full of big houses, all set in beautifully landscaped gardens, which never changed hands for less than a million bucks, and usually much, *much* higher.

The address Sullivan had given Sara, the one where he and Roger were meant to be taking her once they'd picked her up was on Brawner Street and would, she knew, be impressive.

The drive south west had been uneventful, but the traffic was building up, and it had taken some minutes to get off Canal Avenue and to cross the river on Chain Bridge. Looking at the sky, it was going to be another hot but humid day, glutted with gray cloud, the low pressure trough that had been over the city and much of the Eastern Seaboard of the United States for the last few days persisting like a headache over the land that could not be shifted.

They'd also lost the cover of darkness, so she was going to have to find a place to park the Evoque where it wouldn't be noticed and investigated by any overzealous private security guards who would be patrolling McClean. The Evoque was a big car, but an expensive one. It wouldn't look out of place in McClean, but she'd not be able to get Roger to park it just anywhere.

As the car rolled on west now towards McClean, Sullivan was more comfortable. There was still sweat on his brow, and his skin was pale. Roger, driving but still shackled to the wheel. He was playing it cool, but Sara guessed that he was a calculating one. He'd be looking for a way out of this, and he would take any opportunity that presented itself.

A cop car rolled by on the other side of the road, and she saw Roger side eye it. He didn't make any attempt to signal it, but if the same thought had crossed Roger's mind that had just crossed hers it would be the work of a moment to crash the Evoque into a cop car, and Sara would be back on the run, without the Evoque and her sources of information. Even if she killed Roger, she'd be out of the frying pan and into the fire.

Sara pointed to a side road coming up through the trees. "Go up there and stop." They were three miles still from Mc-Clean, but her worry that Roger would try something crazy the closer they got to their destination meant she had to act. The road led up through the trees to a large property she could only glimpse. If luck was with her, she'd be done and dusted here, and they could be back on the road. She unlocked Roger from the steering wheel, and with the Glock in his kidneys, walked him to the tailgate. She handcuffed him again behind his back and opened the first flight case taking out two more pairs of cuffs, a black ski-mask and some rope.

The ski-mask was the same design as the one worn by her attacker in the locker room, and it occurred to her then that Roger was of a similar height and build. She'd already been told by Sullivan that Roger had beaten the woman in the Subaru within a millimeter of her life, so it followed, he'd also had attacked her in the Special Service Center.

What a catch for a gal Roger was turning out to be.

With the ski-mask back to front on his head, she pushed him into the back of the Evoque. It would be cramped with the flight cases but needs must.

She handcuffed Roger's feet together, and then affixed the chain between them to an inner door rest. There was a tartan blanket there, and she covered him over with it.

"You're dead the moment you step into that house. You know that don't you?" his muffled voice came from under the blanket.

"Yeah, maybe. But it's not going to stop me trying."

Sara went to the back seat, threw another blanket over Sullivan, who was still handcuffed to the inner door, and got in the driver's seat, activating all the child locks in the vehicle.

She turned the Evoque around and headed out onto the road.

Right into the path of the police car which had passed them on Chain Bridge.

* * * * *

Cody saw the first of Brant's band of fighters as he loped across the scrub with the lightest strides, keeping a clump of mesquite between him and where he'd suspected they'd be hiding, waiting for the go signal.

The mercenary was crawling towards the church elbow over elbow. As Cody had predicted, they were sending someone forward to look at possible points of entry. The guy carrying out the reconnaissance would then report back, and the final plans would be made. Cody had always enjoyed being the one to do this. Operating alone, with just his eyes and ears backed up by his skills at moving stealthily across rough ground with little cover. This guy—if he was the best Brant and Vick had for the job—was already making a hash of it. Cody had seen the light from the church reflecting off the goggles around his tactical helmet. He wasn't an amateur, but he obviously was the kind of soldier who had more blind self-confidence in himself than the smarts to back it up. Those soldiers who couldn't stand the discipline of remaining in the services but were happy to sell their proficiency to the highest bidder—someone like Brant—often had, in Cody's experience more self-confidence than was safe.

And so it proved here. Cody got within two feet of the camouflage painted guy before he turned and saw him. His eyes had less than a quarter of a second to recognize that someone had got the drop on him, before the butt of the KSG pulped his nose, sending his head back with a snap, and into the land of sweet dreams.

In the mercenaries' pack Cody found tactical zip-ties and secured the unconscious man where he lay. He also retrieved an old battered pair of Pulsar Edge night vision goggles that had seen better days, but were still in working order, a wide bladed Bowie knife, a chunky, rubberized multi-channel radio and a stick of camouflage paint.

Jack smeared the paint onto his face, put on the tactical helmet, slipping the Pulse Edge goggles to the brim. He pulled them down over his eyes, turned them on, and rolled the focus wheel. Scanning the area west of the church, looking back towards the road, he could see the Humvee, but there was no movement around it.

And so, he went hunting again.

Two more mercenaries, some two hundred yards further back Cody took out with minimum fuss. They'd been laying in the sand for some time, and their reflexes were not a match for him, and he left them both zip-locked and unconscious in the scrub, sleeping off brain numbing blows to the head. The KSG might have been a fantastic shotgun, but it was becoming an even more efficient club.

Thousands of years in the evolution of weaponry, and here Cody was taking it right back to the Stone Age. He grinned to himself as he took out the fourth of Brant's men, leaving the actor himself, Vick, Sharon and two more of the not so fortunate-soldiers-of-fortune left. They would, he guessed, be further back again. Perhaps all of them would be together.

"Yow there, Carly, come back? Is that you moving back

towards us mate? Did you get to the church?"

The two-way radio crackled with Vick's voice. He didn't sound overly concerned but they had obviously caught sight of Cody moving through the scrub, which was PITA. If they were now following his progress, he wasn't going to be able to sneak up on them anymore.

He was going to have to take a more direct route.

He waved his hand, and held the radio to his ear, and shook his head.

"Cheap Jap crap." Vick said from the radio. "Come back and report. But for Christ's sake, stay low."

Jack gave the thumbs up, and moved off again in the darkness, crouched low.

The goggles still hadn't told him where Brant, Vick or the others were—but he figured they must have been far enough away from them only to be able to see his some of his silhouette blacked out by the church.

The NVD goggles would have struggled to cope with getting any serious definition in the image because of the bright illumination bleed—so as he moved forward, he made sure he kept the church fully behind him at all times. That meant he would be able to look clearly forward, but Vick and the other's vision would be impaired.

When he'd gone another fifty or so yards, Vick's voice whispered from the radio again. "Mark? Dimitri? Anyone? Christ alive these radios are shit. Can anyone at all hear me out there?"

Looking forward, Cody at last caught sight of Brant and

the others. They were in a hollow six hundred yards from the church, equidistant between the Humvee and their target.

Jack shook his head—for all the great-I-am Brant and Vick had projected in Dry Mouth PD, they weren't that sharp, and they had substandard or old equipment. That gave Cody more confidence, and satisfaction that he'd made the right choice going out to stop them. They would invariably have made a hash of the whole thing, and then the President, the hostages and his brother would be dead.

Jack moved forward again, but gasped as a foot caught him squarely in the small of his back, a knife point stuck into the side of his neck, and a muscular arm slid around his throat tightening across his Adam's apple.

"And what the shitting hell do we have here?" said Sharon, her hot breath scalding in his ear.

CHAPTER 28

"License and registration please, ma'am."

The cop was in his forties, paunchy and looked like he'd been up all night. In fact, he looked like Sara felt right now. She'd told Sullivan under the blanket in the back seat that if he said anything as the cop approached from his car, on the side of the road where he'd pulled them over, that she would blow his balls off and reload for his brains. Sullivan hadn't said anything.

"Is there a problem, officer? I'm running late and I need to be in the office by six. Got an important meeting."

"License and registration," the cop repeated in his perfunctory tone. Sara didn't know if she'd been stopped because the Evoque had not returned with her last night to the intended destination and whoever was behind all this was using their contacts in the police department to track it down, or if the cop was just tired, and wanted something to liven up his tedious shift before it came to an end.

"I'm sorry, I don't think I have it here with me. I left the house in a hurry because I'm running late...as I said."

It sounded lame before it even came out of her mouth, and she inwardly winced.

"Keep your hands where I can see them and get out of the car please, ma'am."

Sara sighed and smiled weakly, putting on her best demure but submissive housewife in a hurry expression and came out of the car.

The cop had been patrolling on his own and the road they were on now wasn't busy, just the occasional vehicle hissing by on the blacktop.

"Name and address please, ma'am. Without license and registration I'm going to have to run you through the system to see if anything pops out. If you'd had your documents with you, then we might not have had to do that. Let that be a lesson for you. So, let's start with a name."

Sara mumbled indistinctly, hoping the cop would strain forward to hear better. He did.

"I'm sorry?"

"Fourteen eighty-eight," she said a little louder this time.

The cop's eyes widened with recognition. It was all Sara needed. She kicked him between the legs and punched him hard across the chops. The cop went down dazed, and she had his gun, and handcuffs in her hand before he'd been able to lift his head off the ground.

"Guess you were just keeping me here before reinforcements could arrive, hmmm?"

"Listen, lady...I just do as I'm told."

"Do you know who I am?"

"No idea at all. Like I said..."

"You just do as you're told. I get it. That's what they all say to excuse themselves '*I was only following orders.*' My God what are we becoming?"

Sara waited for the road to be clear, and then walked the cop back to his car and stuffed him in the trunk after pulling the shotguns and equipment out and transferring it to the rear of the Evoque, to make it even more cramped than it was already for Roger under the blanket.

She slammed the trunk closed on the cop. *That's three men I've collected in less than twelve hours,* she thought. *I'm going to get myself a reputation.*

She swung the Evoque back onto the road and headed into McClean. The traffic had thinned to almost nothing now. McClean was quiet and serene.

If only the people living there knew what it was hiding.

The reach of these people she was up against was terrifying. They could get cops to stop and arrest whoever they wanted. They could get inside any federal facility they liked. They could kill with impunity and they were about to spread their hate across the country in around three hours from now.

Three hours to stop something so massive and dangerous it could tear down a whole country—and Sara still had no idea who was behind it and more importantly what she was going to be able to do to stop them.

＊ ＊ ＊ ＊ ＊

Jack felt the point of Sharon's knife pierce the skin over his left carotid artery. The three quarters of an inch of skin and flesh above the artery feeding blood to his brain and his face was now a little closer to the knife, and a little further away from safety.

That Sharon knew exactly where to point the knife to ensure that he didn't move was troubling, but the fact she hadn't already sliced him open at least gave Cody some hope that there was a way out of this.

He just didn't know what that was yet.

"What have you done with Carly and the others? I checked those radios over myself. There's nothing wrong with them. If they're not answering, then those three boys are out of commission. Please, if you don't want to be dead, tell me my boys aren't dead either."

Jack moved his chin to indicate Sharon needed to lessen the pressure on his windpipe with the other hand before he'd be able to confirm or deny anything.

She loosened the grip slightly but moved the blade another fraction into his flesh. Cody felt a trickle of blood well up around the knife point and move across his skin.

"They'll have headaches, and they're tied up, but they're gonna be ok."

Sharon pushed the knife in a little further. "Okay. That might keep you alive a bit longer, but as you can imagine I'm more than a little pissed off with you. Taking three of our boys out means our rescue mission is compromised badly."

"Badly? Surely it's over...it was the craziest scheme I've ever heard of. Brant's insane."

"The rich are never insane, Cody, they're eccentric."

She took the knife away from his neck after the arm around his neck was replaced with a pistol in the small of his back. "Now crawl, you prick. I'm pretty sure my boss is going to want to have words with you."

It didn't begin with words. It began with a punch to the gut. Then another, and when Brant moved away to cradle his fist because he'd hurt it punching Cody so hard, Vick buried two pile drivers into Cody's gut. This all happened while the guy Brant called Boxer, held both Cody's elbows from behind in a death-grip, digging his nails into Cody's skin, drawing more blood to compliment the line of it drying stiffly on his neck.

They'd retreated back away from the church to the Humvee. Two of the remaining mercenaries had been sent to look for their three comrades and bring them back for conference and to reset the mission.

The punching and the insults seemed just to be a way to pass the time until the others came back.

Jack sagged but wasn't allowed to fall, which he would have done if Boxer had let go of him.

Sharon slapped his face hard to open his eyelids. Cody was glad the knife had been sheathed, but her eyes looked like could slice his throat open with just a glance.

"You've ruined everything," Brant said like a kid talking to his father because he'd grounded him for the week.

Jack gasped with the pain in his gut. He knew how to take a punch there to protect himself with his muscles, but the punches from Vick had been cruel and jarring. He felt like he was going to throw up yesterday's breakfast, and pretty much everything he'd eaten for the last six months. "I saved all your lives Brant...I'm just one man, and I took three of your guys out on my own...How do you think you would have fared with the Agents and SWAT team in the church?"

"Yeah, you're quite good," said Sharon. "But you still got taken out by a girl."

Jack spat bloody phlegm from his mouth, caused by the punch to his gut mixing with the bleeding from the inside of his mouth from where Sharon had slapped him. "Yeah, your friend Vick punches like a girl too."

Vick roared and buried another flashing fist in Cody's belly. He was ready for it. Knew it was coming but it still stunned him. What he had learned though at the expense of the punch about Vick's character would be invaluable if he was going to get out of this. Vick was quick to anger and couldn't resist retaliation.

Jack put that down in his mental armory. Play the man, not the football.

Vick punched him again and pulled his head back by his hair. "Yow know I could just shoot yow now, and leave yow in a ditch for the feds to find after we've rescued your dickhead President, don't you?"

Jack couldn't nod because of how hard Vick was holding

his head, so he just said, "Sure. I guess shooting and punching people while your friends hold them steady for you is just your level. I reckon Sharon's the best man of the lot of you."

Sharon laughed. "Quite right too."

Vick boiled but he let go of Cody's hair. Brant stepped forward again. "Now Mister Cody, I won't have murder committed under my name, but you have to admit you present us with a problem. You have wasted valuable time, you have hurt my men, and now you're doing your best to rile my friends. I would suggest we just agree to differ on what should be done to rescue the President and leave it as that, yes?"

Jack took a breath and tried to ignore the nausea bubbling up from his stomach. "I don't think you mean any of that do you, Brant? I think you've seen an opportunity where you can advance your brand. Win or lose here today—President dead or President saved—you're on a winner. Your stock is going to rise and you're going to be seen as the man who tried when the government hesitated."

Brant smiled. "Oh, do you think so? I really hadn't seen it that way at all."

Jack looked from Vick to Sharon. "He doesn't care if you get through this at all, as long as he gets his face in the spotlight."

"Shut your mouth," said Vick, making fists. "Brant might not want yow dead, but I really do."

The five mercenaries had returned to the Humvee now. Three with bloody faces, broken noses and blood in their hair from Cody's handiwork. The three who'd been released looked sheepish and embarrassed. Vick pointed at Cody.

"This long streak of piss took yow all out on his own, and it took a bloody bird to bring him down. I should shoot the blood lot of yow."

Brant shook his head. "Let's defer any punishment until altered we've rescued the President, but as a thank you, I think I'll give you all a little treat before we regroup."

Jack fixed Brant with a hard stare. The movie star's face was bright and alive. There was an idea forming behind it.

"I'm sure all three of you would like a chance to thank Mister Cody for helping you understand the chinks in your armor. Why don't you have a word with him...personally?"

CHAPTER 29

The house had been built from brick in the colonial Georgian style, with a steeply pitched roof, and double paired chimneys that rose almost as high from the roof as their bases might have been measured from the ground.

Much of the back of the beautiful house was hidden by a huge, shaggy, Atlas cedar which dominated a hedged formal garden, with a sunken Italian stone fish pool, and a riot of high summer flowers.

There was a hill behind the house which Sara had climbed as inconspicuously as she could. There was no property on top of the hill, so she wouldn't be overlooked from above, and there was enough tree and bush cover for her to make it to her vantage point unseen.

Sara had parked the Evoque off a quiet access road half a mile away, backing it between two bushes, beneath a broad oak. It wasn't exactly hidden and might have passed for a vehicle parked while the owner took their dog for a walk in the woods clothing the Pimmit Hills.

Sara had brought a bag from the back of the Evoque with Kevlar vest, an MP5, spare magazines and a clutch of grenades. She had no idea if she was going to need them, but today could go any of a thousand ways.

She scanned the back of the huge house with field glasses from the flight case. There was no movement she could see behind the windows. There wasn't even a light on. It occurred to her that Sullivan might not have been telling the truth, but Roger's reaction to Sullivan's admissions were still enough to convince her he had been on the level. And he must have known. If she came back empty handed, then her supposed skills as a torturer would be employed without delay.

No, this was the house. This was the place and inside, she hoped, was the evidence she needed to convince whoever she could find who was still trustworthy that the republic was in danger equivalent to any that had it come up against in the past.

The lack of movement or activity in and around the house however was troubling. Perhaps whoever had been waiting for her had moved on when she hadn't shown up with Roger and Sullivan. Alternatively, they might be in rooms at the front of the house she couldn't yet see. Whatever the truth of what was going on in the house, there was only one way for Sara to find out.

Sara had dispensed with the baseball cap and her overcoat, slipping the tactical vest around her, and covering her head and the whiteness of her face and blondeness of her hair with the ski-mask. She'd put her hands into black shooting gloves and covered her sneakers in damp mud to take the visibility of them down. Once she was ready, she moved out.

There was enough cover to get her to the security fence at the back of the house pretty much without being seen by anyone who wasn't already looking for her.

The fence was chain link, held a sign to say *Keep Out Private Property*, but didn't appear to have any overt security cameras or other measures to dissuade intruders. That didn't mean there weren't any early warning systems at play here—but had no choice but to continue.

The flight cases had again thrown up all manner of useful tools too. The spring-loaded wire cutters made short work of the chain link. If she had tripped an alarm, no one had come running from the house, and there were no signs of snarling dogs or other sounds of alarm.

She shook her head. Was this the complacency of these people writ large? So sure of themselves that they could and would not be touched, they kept their security to normal neighborhood levels.

It seemed insane, but there had been other indications that they might not be as invincible and ahead of the game as they first might appear. Roger might have been a sadistic killer in the making, but he'd flubbed the Subaru woman's murder, and they'd had to resort to the sledgehammer of a bomb blast to make sure she didn't talk.

Then there was Sullivan. The guy was a complete putz. Breaking his finger had made him almost cry like a child.

If you're going to send someone to take out a CIA agent like Sara—and they must have known a little about her and her capabilities, then you'd send someone better than him to accompany Roger.

The fence breached, Sara ran to the hedge line.

There were twisted topiary animals and figures there that looked like they hadn't been tended to for a long time. Certainly not since the beginning of the summer. Now that she could observe the garden close up, it was clear that it hadn't been cleared or swept back for longer than you'd expect of a McClean property.

She moved along the hedge row keeping as low as she could without impeding her forward progress, but she made sure her eyes swept back and forth of the windows. She detected no movements behind the black squares of glass. It was if the house was dead.

The back entrance was set at the bottom of three well-worn stone steps. Mud and the detritus of leaf mulch from the season before had silted up around the foot to the door. It didn't look like it had been opened for months.

There were two windows in the door and Sara put her eye against one of them to see what was beyond. A short stone flagged corridor leading to a white painted door with a big iron lock was all she could see. The walls were lumpy, the plaster covering them in need of replacement. Cobwebs hung in dusty hammocks from the ceiling and the corners of the corridor. It spoke, like the door and the garden of neglect.

The back door was, of course, locked.

One thing she hadn't found in the flight case was a lock picking kit and she was annoyed that she'd never got herself one like Jack Cody had in his boots. If she was going to open this door, she was going to have to force it, because there was no way she'd be willing to shoot the lock.

She began to look around for a convenient lever to shove between the jamb and the lock, but had to push herself into the wall, as a sash window ten feet away from the door was pushed up with a loud crash.

Jack could taste blood and dirt.

He was picked up from the ground for what felt like the hundredth time and slammed again into the side of the Humvee. As he fell back, he could see the door was slick with blood. His blood. He hurt in so many places, it wasn't possible to tell exactly where the blood was coming from. And to be honest, as he crashed down, he was only thinking about it to take the mind off the beating he was getting.

It was easier to cope with if he was thinking about something else.

"Ok, I've seen enough," said Brant. "Tie him up and put him in the truck. We can dump him at a hospital later when we've got this thing done."

Hands pulled him to his feet again but for the first time after a beating that seemed to have lasted for a geological time scale, Cody was not punched or kicked again. His hands were tied, his ankles too, and he was thrown onto the floor of the Humvee with a thud that removed the first unhindered breaths he'd been able to pull into his lungs since human ancestors had given up the sea.

He lay in the hot dark. Head spinning, limbs aching. He was a bruise with a body attached, but thankfully nothing felt like it was broken. He was having difficulty breathing through his nose—they'd punched him on it a good couple of times—but right now he wasn't sure if it was because it was broken, or if he'd hit the ground face first so many times is nostrils were clogged with bits of desert.

Brant and the others had withdrawn to hold a conference. They were well out of earshot, but even with the windows closed, Cody could hear the rumble of an argument. He hoped what he'd said about Brant had had at least some impact on the others and that they too had worked out that something was stinking in the state of Denmark. Cody also knew that if the mercenaries were true to their breed, all Brant would have to do to change their minds would be to double or triple their fee. If they pulled off the mission, he'd be good for the cash for sure.

Feeling was returning to his bones, and his heart was starting to slow to a manageable level. They'd hogtied his wrists to his ankles, and ordinarily that would have taken most people out of action.

But not Cody. The hogtie gave the added bonus of getting his hands next to his heels.

It was suddenly like Christmas behind his back.

In a matter of moments, he had the compartment open, and the plastic edged razor blade in his palm. It wouldn't be prudent to do anything with it just yet, not until he was sure the argument had ended, and Brant's people had moved off towards the church. Then, Cody thought to himself, he was going to have to go after them all over again—and this with the added problem of being beaten all to hell.

David had had the right idea in career choice, me...not so much. Cody thought wryly.

And that thought froze in his head as a bullet smashed the side window of the Humvee, whizzed across to the other side and blew out the window in the opposite door. Cody was covered in crushed glass from his head to his backside. Pieces of it ran down the back of his neck, and into the whorls of his ear.

Shaking his head to get the glass out from hair and ear, he began sawing at his bonds with the razor.

Had the argument turned to a gunfight? Surely not. But he could hear shouting now and someone screaming.

Brant. "I'm hit! I'm hit!"

Vick. "Get down! Take cov..."

The whistle of another bullet cutting him off mid-sentence, groan of a dying man and a big body thudding to the earth.

Jack's feet were free, and he set about working on the rope around his wrists.

Sharon was shouting. "Sniper! There's a bleedin' sniper! Out there!"

The mercenaries were returning fire and he could hear

them diving for cover. More bullets slammed into the hood of the Humvee, clanging around the engine, causing a hiss of escaping liquid under pressure or vapor. Two more bullets smashed into the side of the Humvee at the rear. One a little high, and the next one was lower down the vehicle. The side of the gold and diamond encrusted Humvee rattled and shook, and a third bullet made a tire explode with a cracking concussion that made the chassis tilt and joggle.

Dammit, thought Cody. Those are rounds from the sniper. He's going for the fuel tank to blow this sucker up, and I'm sitting right on top of the reservoir.

His hands came free and, trying to forget the protesting agony of his beaten body, Cody opened the door on the opposite side of the Humvee and pushed the door open.

He was blown out of the vehicle on a gust of flame as the burning detonation of the fuel tank tore upwards and around the car. He hit the dirt with a painful thud and began rolling— away from the Humvee—in case his hair or clothes were on fire. Then he was up and running.

Four seconds into his desperate sprint the ammo or explosives or both that were in the Humvee's trunk went up like a MOAB in a sewer. It seemed like the whole night had been lit up, the bowl of blue dark above his head turned into a negative image. A gust of hot wind, a rush of dust and torn vegetation knocked him off his feet again and set Cody barreling into another depression in the landscape.

Head over heels and side to side he fell, down fifteen or so yards of stony earth, and prickly plants until he slashed into a near dry creek and lay there, on his back in the six inches of water, looking at the bits of flaming car that had been blown into the sky and were now raining down around him.

A burning seat with all its metal floor plate fixing crash landed not two feet from his body. He flinched sideways as more bits of near atomized Humvee clattered into the earth, some pieces rolling down the same incline as he had into the water. A golden wheel, still with half a tire attached, spun through the air like a giant's coin toss, and threw up a welter of spray from the insubstantial trickle of the creek.

A large round object, sailed over the lip of the incline, hit the slope, bounced once and battered Cody between the thighs.

Everything went quiet.

Jack couldn't even hear anything still burning. It was if the explosion from the Humvee's armaments had been so large, it had simply blown itself out.

Jack sighed. The water was soothing on his injuries and cool against his back. But he couldn't stay here however enticing the thought might have been at that time.

With a groan and a body that felt like it was creaking like a bicycle left to rot in the garden all winter, Cody hauled himself up into a sitting position.

"Oh man…" he said as he looked between his legs and saw the half charred, open eyed, with its jaw torn away and lord knew from where, head of Brant Stevens.

CHAPTER 30

Sara pressed herself back into the doorway not daring to breathe, trying to think herself thinner than she was already. If whoever was at the window, looked out and down, Sara would be seen. She gingerly drew her Glock from her belt and made ready to shoot her way out of here if she had to.

Something flew from the window and Sara flinched involuntarily, raising the gun, putting pressure on the trigger.

A moth eaten and saggy ginger tom cat landed on the grass, looked indignantly back at the window and hissed at it.

"Oh, shaddap, you mangy piece of shit!" A man's voice. American. "You can come in tonight if you're lucky. And if you spray in the house one more time, I'll tear your balls off myself with me teeth."

The cat turned its back on the scolding and walked away. Tail flicking imperiously. The window was slammed shut, but crucially for Sara, she didn't hear it being bolted or locked in place.

The cat took a look at Sara as it walked past, but as she didn't look like someone who was good for food or fussing, it moved on again without a second glance.

Sara pulled the ski-mask from her face. She was hot, the blood was thudding through her temples, and the adrenaline was racing her anxiety all around her heart.

She waited sixty seconds, hopped out of the depression near the back corridor, and edged towards the window. The gloomy though warm and humid day meant there was a lack of sunshine. If there had it might have picked her out against the russet brickwork for anybody watching from up on the hill. She had to move fast, because even with the gloom, she was too exposed here and felt it.

The mid-section of the window was in line with her shoulder, so she'd have no problem looking in. Although it was a dull day, there was still a lot reflection on the window. It made her have to put her face close up to see through the glass into the room beyond.

There were dusty looking armchairs and oil paintings on the wall of long forgotten men and their horses. Someone in a tricorn hat pointing to the hills. Some Piscataway standing proudly outside their tipis. A marble fireplace that would have shamed the one in Charles Foster Kane's Xanadu at the far end. The room looked large enough to play an NBA game in it yet still leave room for an MLB diamond and cheerleaders.

But of the voice that hated the cat, there was no sign of the human it belonged to.

Sara pushed up the sash and the window slid up easily,

holding in place. Throwing the gun bag through and following it in, Sara closed the window and looked about. The room smelled musty and unused, just like the garden of the house had looked close up.

Thinking about it, that made a lot of sense. If the house was ostensibly empty and had been for a while, what better place to use as a base of operations—especially if you were going to bring captives back for interrogation and some rough stuff?

Sara moved into the room proper.

Against a wall was a long and elegantly proportioned 18th century George III mahogany sideboard. There was one center drawer and two flanking cabinets, with gilt brass pulls that hadn't been cleaned for some time. There was a layer of dust on top of the sideboard that expressed the same level of neglect as all she had seen so far. This made her all the more sure that her assessment of the use of the residence was exactly as she thought.

She opened one of the side cabinets in the sideboard. She took a grenade from the bag plus several magazines for the MP5. She clipped them to the utility belt, and after stuffing the bag into the sideboard, clicking the door closed, she prepared to leave the room. There was no point carrying everything around with her and one grenade will cause more than enough damage in here if she needed it to.

Sara placed her ear against the door leading to the interior of the house. There was no sound coming through the wood, and whoever had the problem with the cat certainly wasn't walking about outside.

She opened the door a crack.

The floors in the hallway beyond were dusty and there was a little left to be kicked around by whoever was present. There were three doors leading off the corridor, and antique furniture with empty Chinese vases on top of occasional tables, pictures of the great and good from another time filling the space.

Sara ducked back behind the door as she heard a loud creak— then realized it had come from the ceiling over the corridor, towards the front of the house. She opened the door wider.

More creaks. In two places at least pointing to two, possibly three people upstairs.

She moved out into the corridor, skimming along the wall, around the tables and floor vases, MP5 at the ready.

The stairs were wide and wooden. She took them two at a time, but fleet of foot. Although the stairs were old, they were sturdy and well made. They weren't covered in cobwebs nor looked neglected, so this was a heavy traffic area of the house.

Sara arrived on a landing.

This part of the house had a corridor that had no natural light of its own. A bulb without a shade burned halfway down its length throwing desultory light. From one of the doors there came another creak, a thud and a groan. Indistinct voices from at least three people could be heard discussing something, but not clear enough to pick out any detail.

Sara hefted the submachine gun and went sideways along the wall to the door behind which the voices were emanating.

The floorboard beneath her right foot creaked so loud, it sounded like an opening door.

Footsteps came thudding towards the door and an irritated male voice said, "If Raymond has let that damned cat in here again, I'm going to neuter them both!"

Before Sara could turn and get out of the way, the door opened on a man with the sleeves of his sweater rolled up and blood streaked all the way to his elbows like a butcher at his block.

The Butcher was in his forties, black haired with a buzz cut that had reduced the hair on the side of his head to mere bristles. He seemed to have too much face for his features. Mouth, nose and eyes were crowded in the middle of his face like three islands in a fleshy sea.

"Get that freaking cat…oh."

Sara's gun was pointing at the man's gut. Her finger was on the trigger. Butcher raised his hands and stepped back into the room.

Covering him, Sara followed. The room has half as large as the one where she had entered the house and situated on the front range. There were closed drapes over all the windows, and another shade-less bulb hung from the ceiling.

The room had the same mix of antique furniture, oil paintings and Chinese vases she'd seen in the rest of the house.

But here, as well as the Butcher, there were two other people standing. A man in his fifties in a marine's uniform, complete with colonel's braids, a beret and a chest full of medals. His face was a mask of shock at seeing Sara. Next to him was a woman. She was mid-thirties perhaps, blonde with a face so sharp Sara could have shaved her legs on it. Sharp and the Marine both raised their hands too.

"I know you're not going to move, but I'll say the obligatory *nobody move,* just to make sure we're all on the same page," Sara said, taking two more steps forward.

Between them, tied to a chair was a man who was in the process of being beaten to death.

Blood streamed from his mouth, his eyes were puffy and black. His head came up from his chest and his gaze fixed Sara through her appalled core.

The bloody man's eyes widened.

His eyes implored Sara and as he struggled against his bonds, his slack mouth clicked up lips forming two words that came out like a rattling exhalation rather than a sentence. "Behind you," he breathed.

✳ ✳ ✳ ✳ ✳

The Humvee was surrounded by burned bodies.

Not one of the mercenaries or their leaders had survived the explosion which had torn through them like a chainsaw through bamboo.

The Humvee was utterly destroyed, and as Cody crawled low through the brush towards the blackened hull the first lightening of the darkness at the lip of the eastern horizon could be seen beyond Dry Mouth.

He scanned the ground as best he could, looking for whatever vantage point the sniper had used to shoot Brant and Vick, and then explode the Humvee.

Jack was not able, as yet, to pick out the buildings on the edge of Dry Mouth, but the sniper couldn't be there. His accuracy had been woeful when he'd been shooting at Cody on his headlong rush across the rooftops, and he'd been as close to Cody as a roof on the other side of the street.

Brant and the others had been taken out three hundred yards or more beyond the church. Even a static target would have presented too many targeting variables to a part-time amateur. No, the sniper was nearer. He—or she—had made it out of Dry Mouth when the troops and federal agents has been forced to withdraw into the town along main street and was probably hiding somewhere on a slight rise within two hundred yards or less of Cody's present location.

The sniper would have a night sight, more ammunition and the certainty he could move freely in the vicinity of the church now the area had been cleared.

He'd taken out Brant and the Humvee and there was a good chance the sniper might have thought they had taken out Cody too.

The bullets blasted into the Humvee suggested Cody might have been one of the primary targets. Perhaps, in his rush to get out of town and intercept Brant and the others, the sniper had followed him using NVD goggles.

Jack scratched his head and closed his eyes.

As if things weren't bad enough with the situation in the church, what the hell did they need a sniper for to muddy the waters?

The answer, or course, when he let go of his annoyance was quite simple. If the people on the inside the church, had an agent on the outside, keeping them informed of what was going on, and cleaning up for them, their position would be even more secure.

Their confidence would, quite simply, be bulletproof.

A man like Elkins would enjoy having someone on the outside stirring things up.

There were scorched and ruined weapons all around the Humvee that he could see in the grass and singed scrub. He found a Bowie knife with a half melted rubber handle. A Colt Government 1911A just beyond the circle of crisply burned earth. The magazine came out ok, and the shells were in intact. When he put the magazine back in and racked the gun, the action moved the first shell into the chamber.

It would do for now.

Of the KSG and the Diamondback there was no sign.

Everything else—the radios, the NVDs and any other equipment was burned beyond all recognition amongst the corpses.

Jack ached000002 and took a moment to wish along with the Colt, he'd found a treasure chest full of Advil to quell his protesting body, but painkillers were going to have to wait.

Moving again on his elbows through the scrub, he struck out towards the church. As ever, he kept low, hoping against hope the sniper didn't spot him. There would be times when the ground would undulate steeply, and he'd find himself on higher ground.

He was moving towards the dawn rather than away from it and that might illuminate him as well as the spotlights playing on the church. Black camouflage paint was still sticky on his face. The beating he'd taken hadn't cleaned it all off so that was a small plus.

It took fifteen minutes of painful and difficult movement to get himself near enough to the church for what he wanted to achieve.

All the arc lights were playing at the front of the church. If there had been any spotlights illuminating the rear of the building, they had either been shot out, or their generators, left to their own devices by the retreating federal forces, had failed at some point during the night.

The back wall was clapboard construction like the rest of the church. There were only two small windows high up, behind which there didn't seem to be any light shining. The glass in the frames was dark and unrevealing. There were enough hostiles in there to place sentries at those windows, and perhaps there were guys in there who would be back soon. But Cody's vision was acute enough to see that right now, at least, there was no one looking out of them.

Jack had a decision to make.

His plan had been to use the church as a cover shadow—it was the only thing on the landscape between him and Dry Mouth.

And he had to get back to Dry Mouth. Had to.

There was no time to walk out west, and circle around on the desert road. That would take at least an hour or more. He would have to take the direct route back into the town, and that meant going past the church. But which side to break for? Was the sniper watching from the right side or the left?

Jack didn't know.

It was a coin toss, and he was desperate to get back to town so that he could find someone he could trust to talk to about a plan that was forming in his mind.

That was until the shooting began from inside the church.

CHAPTER 31

Plaster and splinters littered down from the ceiling.

The hostages ducked, cowering where they sat. The President had thrown a protective arm across the first lady and Sandra had her hands over her ears.

Jud lowered his gun and spoke into the radio. "Hacker, I don't care about logistical problems. You will bring my daughter here before eight AM or so help me *Jesus* I'm going to send the President to hell in a blaze of terrible glory."

Hacker's voice came from the radio. "Mister Elkins, we've given you all that you've asked for. We've given you food, drink, and moved the exclusion zone back a full mile as you ordered. But you have given us nothing. Not one thing. And now you're asking for your daughter to be released from a federal facility where she is being held, and still you're not willing to move."

"This is not a negotiation, Hacker. This is an order. You get her here, or the next bullets go into the first lady. And as for Kevin's promise you weren't going to attack, if we hadn't stopped those assholes you sent in the Humvee, you'd all be sorry right now, because the dead Presidents wouldn't just be on your dollar bills."

"I assure you those men had nothing to do with us, Elkins, that was an entirely unauthorized action by persons unknown. My men are investigating. You didn't want anyone in the exclusion zone, and we haven't put anyone in there. We have stood by our word. Please believe me."

"How can I believe you, Hacker? Your lips are moving!"

Jud clicked off the radio and turned on President Harwood. "Can you believe this guy? Doesn't he want to save you? Doesn't he want to get you and your good lady wife out of this mess?"

Harwood's face was a blank mask, his voice low and colorless. "Even I'm bored waiting, Elkins. This timetable you've been set by your lords and masters is just bullshit, you know that, right?"

Jud leaned on McDaniel's coffin, resting the side of his head on his fist and regarded the President quizzically. Even he thought it was odd hearing such language from the mouth of the Commander in Chief.

"I guess your choice of language just shows how far this country has sunk, Harwood. How can anyone have faith in a head of state who would speak in such a way? Where's your dignity, man? Where's your sense of respect for the office of President? Whilst you're wiping your dirty feet on the constitution, some of us have been planning on making America into what it used to be. That shining beacon on the hill."

Harwood shook his head. "You? Make something of the country you're trying to break with your actions? With your bullshit plans? As a person, I don't matter, but you've put a noose around the neck of this office. How does that fix anything? There will be a President after me, and another after him. You, Elkins, you'll just be a passing second on the clockface of history."

Jud felt the anger rising up in him again. "You might think that with your politics you're changing things—but you change *nothing*. There are still poor. There are still immigrants swarming over our borders, stealing the jobs from good Americans, seeing what handouts they can twist out of the fine, good upstanding..."

"White," cut in Harwood. "Don't forget white."

"Damn straight Mister President. How many of the founding fathers of this great nation were Mexican? Hmmm?"

Pavlina put her hand on Harwood's arm. "Darling. Don't..."

Harwood rounded on Pavlina. "Darling is it? Darling? You call me darling *now*? That's rich. Coming in here you didn't even want to hold my hand, and now I'm your *darling*. And that's not because I'm standing up for what's right. You don't care what's right—you just want to keep things calm so that these psychotic assholes don't shoot you!"

The hostages gasped at the President's words and Pavlina shrank away, her expression one of crushed disappointment. David and the Reverend Just looked up from where they were sitting, their faces concerned. Sandra and Bo laughed and looked at Jud. "Hey, baby, looks like they're human after all!"

Harwood thumped his fist down on his knee and Henri jumped, his lugubrious face quivering with surprise.

"You people. You d*amnable* people. You don't like the way things are run so you take a gun to it. A bomb to it. If you so want to change things, why don't you make the hard choices? Educate yourselves, become representatives for your communities, give the people you want to represent a voice—not just the sound of bullets."

Jud came away from the coffin pointing back at it and the picture of McDaniel.

"Jefferson McDaniel. Korean and Vietnam War veteran. A hero by all accounts. If his medals are anything to go by, that is. A life of political service and a reputation built on sobriety, sound judgement and a moral compass a nation could steer itself by. He's so revered, even the President wanted to come to his funeral. But tell me, Mister President—what did McDaniel achieve? Hmm? What did he change by playing the game by the rules?"

Harwood almost spat the words out that if they had been bullets, Jud would be a dead man. "He *served*. That's what he did."

"And again. I ask, what did serving this corrupt country achieve? Hmm? What did your precious democracy do while McDaniel was part of the system? Are there any less poor people today? Are there any less injustices against the white race? Is there any less of a glass ceiling for us to break through? When everyone else is put in the line before us, don't be surprised when we jump the queue."

Jud was warming to the speech now. He strode imperiously up the aisle towards Harwood. "You see men like me like a dog sees its fleas. You scratch at us, you use chemicals to eradicate us, you try to drown us. You leave us to starve. You do all those things to your *own* people—and it doesn't matter if you're Democrat or Republican—you're all the same. The system you've created works for all of you and kills the rest of us."

"You don't need to do this to make a difference, Elkins. You don't need to kill us to get things done."

"It all depends what I want to get done, doesn't it?"

The silence boomed. The moment hung there like a jewel Jud could just pluck it out of the air, put it in his pocket, and take out to marvel at whenever he wanted.

"Just tell me, Mister President. If I hadn't had you here as a completely captive audience, would I *ever* have got the chance, the real chance, to tell you any of this to your face?"

Harwood blinked and hesitated. Then he sighed. "No, I don't suppose you would."

Jud ruffled the President's hair and stood back like a painter admiring the picture he'd just finished.

"Then I guess I changed *that*." He opened his arms wide. "And it's just a start of the whole lot of listening you and your kind will have to do from now on. We have found *our* voice, and we are going to speak!"

CHAPTER 32

Sara ducked and the bullets from the gun behind her went over her head, smashing the glass in the windows behind the drapes.

She propelled herself backwards and caught her shoulder under the gun arm of whoever was behind her, as another volley of shots spat along the wall like stitches.

A painting was cut across the center and the containing frame, released from centuries of taut service, clattered to the floor in a welter of dust.

Sara sent her elbow backwards in a savage short stab. The resultant cry told her the trajectory of her arrowed arm had hit the guy straight in his marriage license.

Sara fell onto her ass and fired up and over her shoulder. The MP5 bucked in her hands. Bullets blew chunks out of the ceiling, tore apart the doorframe and with a surprised gasp, carved a furrow down the face of the man who'd tried to kill her. He fell backwards, spraying blood and bone, crashing back through the doorway, his feet twitching, semi-automatic SIG-Sauer still in his hand.

Sara pointed the MP5 at the Butcher, Sharp and Marine who were now trying to scrape the ceiling with their fingertips. "Move back, now. Away from him."

They did as they were told, kept going backwards until the wall arrested their progress.

"Now what the hell is going on here? You…" she indicated Marine, "…if that uniform is real, and those medals are earned, what the blue blazes are you involved in, man?"

Marine said nothing. His face was white. Butcher looked down at the carpet. Sharp fixed Sara with a steely gaze that at least showed she had some backbone, or the overconfidence to affect some.

It was Sharp who broke the moment with sinewy threat. "You have no idea what you've got yourself mixed up in Sara *Durell*. No idea at all. Don't think you can stop us with that pop gun you have in your hands. Because if you do think that, then you are sadly mistaken."

"Sara…" the guy in the chair said. He coughed and a spray of blood came out on his breath in a fine mist. He had severe internal injuries by the looks of it, and it was his blood all over the Butcher's arms.

It was then a bolt of recognition struck Sara's memory. She knew this man. It was Denis Barber…the intelligence analyst from the Special Activities Center. The guy who'd kept bringing her coffees, the guy who had spoken to Subaru Woman first, and then passed the call to Sara.

"Denis...?" she stepped forward and, still covering the others with the MP5, used the cuff of her shirt to wipe some of the congealing blood from his beaten face.

Denis nodded, and spoke with a halting struggle. "I...took the call...gave it to you... they...wanted to know if the woman had...said anything to me...if she'd told me her name...they didn't believe me... I told them the truth...but he...wouldn't stop."

"It's gonna be okay," said Sara. "They've been trying to get me here to find out what I know too. I know the woman didn't tell you anything. She didn't tell me anything." Sara looked up and fixed Sharp and the others with a look that could strip paint. The expression on Sharp and Marine's face—after she'd told Denis she knew nothing, could not hide their relief. So, Sara turned over her ace. "But Sullivan did."

Sharp blinked. Her composure gone.

Marine's mouth *phhhupe*d open.

"Her name was Debbie Langwith and she was the Vice President's Deputy Chief of Staff."

Butcher roared and dropped his arms. The rage on his face twisting his expression into a treble-clef of murder.

He got halfway to Sara before she shot him. He spun, his arms flung wide and his mouth still working a cry of anger and shock, his legs crumpling, his body smashing down in a tangle of arms and legs. He rolled onto his back, and his jaw went slack.

Sara pointed the MP5 at Marine and Sharp. "I'm guessing I only need one of you alive to tell me what's happening and why—so who wants to talk, and who wants to die?"

* * * * *

When Marine had finished—his name was Colonel Marcus Blake—Sara wanted to find a chair to sit on because her legs were turning to Jell-O. But what she did instead was pull down the drape cords, and tied Blake up next to Sharp, whose name, Blake had told Sara was Cortina Lane. It was a name, like Langwith's, which she was familiar with, but could not connect the sharply faced woman to.

Lane hadn't said a word while Blake spilled his guts to avoid being shot. She just looked at Blake with disappointment and hatred.

Blake had told Sara that the broadcast was scheduled for 11.10 a.m. That's when the signal would be given, and America would enter its new dark night of its soul.

"Don't tell her anything," Cortina had spat at Blake.

"I'm trying to keep us both alive, woman," Blake spat back. "You might have the suicidal fervor of the ideologue, but I want to get out of this intact. And anyway, it doesn't matter what we tell her. No one will ever believe her. We've seen to that."

Blake had seemed proud about what he went on to tell her about how the army he'd served had become weak, and the new one he'd help mold would be better, stronger and purer of purpose. The members of the New Militia wouldn't be conscripts or mere volunteers, they would feel this in their hearts and in their guts.

Blake's eyes had been wild and dewy. He might not have considered himself an ideologue, but God he believed *this*. All of it. There was a pulse working in his neck that throbbed excitedly. In the end, when he'd told her what was really going on, he'd grinned as Sara's eyes had widened, and she'd almost staggered back a step and put a hand to steady herself on the wall.

Everything she'd worked for and believe in all this time was going to be swept away, and the people doing it weren't a foreign power, they weren't the recognize enemy. They were Americans.

"When fourteen eighty-eight rolls around," Blake whispered, "it'll be curtain up. Make sure you've got a front row seat, Sara. I dare say it's gonna be pretty."

When Blake told her exactly what was about to go down in Dry Mouth, Sara roared and then held the Glock to Blake's temple, unable to listen any longer without reacting. The knuckle of her trigger finger white.

Blake had closed his eyes, flinched, and tried to cower.

Sara almost did it. She almost pulled the trigger and executed the brash, bragging military man without a second thought.

But she had held back. Released the trigger. Stepped back. Wiped her mouth.

Perhaps I don't want to sink to their level, she thought.

It was the best explanation she had, and it would have to suffice until she could examine her motivations any further.

Sara released Denis from the chair, and he slumped to the

floor. He was in a very bad way, and he'd need an emergency room, but Sara knew that she couldn't risk taking him to one. Not now she knew the truth. "You know I have to finish this first, Denis. I can't take you to a hospital. They have eyes and ears everywhere—but if I can deal with this at source, I'll be able to send someone to you. You have my word. Passes were meant to be used."

Denis nodded. He couldn't say anything, but he squeezed her hand. It left a bloody palm print there. With a supreme effort he managed to string one sentence together before slipping into unconsciousness. "Your...turn...to bring the coffee."

Leaving Denis, Sara got up and crossed the room. Cortina's razor-sharp face was white with fury. Sara went down on her haunches and pulled at the knots she'd used to secure the woman and released her arm. Then she stood, and taking the Glock from her belt, pointed it at the woman. "Take your suit and blouse off."

Cortina's expression changed to one of amusement. "You're not my type, darling. Let's just agree I'm flattered but uninterested and move on, shall we?"

Sara fired a bullet into the floorboards next to the woman.

Cortina began taking off her clothes.

When Cortina was tied up again, Sara changed into her suit, put on her mules, and tied her hair up in as close an approximation to Cortina's style as she could. The blouse and skirt were a little tight, but she wasn't too far away from Cortina's figure to make the clothes uncomfortable.

"You won't get past the first level of security. You'll be

stopped and taken, and then we will kill you. Nothing is going to stop the announcement, the death of the President and the second American Revolution."

"Maybe you're right. But I'm going to try."

Sara reached into the pocket of Cortina's suit jacket and pulled out a White House security pass.

"And as to being stopped at security...let's see how far *this* gets me."

CHAPTER 33

Jack tossed the coin in his head.

He would break right.

If he was going to be out in the open, illuminated by the glare of the arc lights, and the dawn that was inching higher in the sky, the subterfuge of keeping to cover wasn't going to help him.

He needed speed and he needed power.

Jack's body protested and moaned as he got up and began to sprint. His legs were like concrete piles sunk in mud. His ribs, the ones that had been fractured, allowed him to breathe but only at a cost of energy- sapping agony.

Jack burst through into the circle of light and he was now fully exposed. The church wall on his right was brushed by his crazily running shadow. A bullet kicked up the sand at his feet.

Dammit.

Wrong side.

He sped on, but another bullet thudded into the earth in front of him, and a ricochet of hot lead stung the back of his hand.

The wound was shallow but was already splitting open to blood. He began to zig-zag, like he had before on the root top. A bullet zinged over his head. Another whistled past, through the air his body had just vacated. There was no chance to stop now. He must carry on.

Left. Right. Left...

The sound of broken glass from the church was followed almost immediately by the clatter of a semi-automatic pistol. Someone from inside the church had seen him and had shot out a window to get at him.

But he was moving fast, away from the front of the church now.

He had a hundred yards to go.

A hundred yards.

He could do it in eleven seconds... he could...

A bullet winged his arm, but it didn't arrest his headlong rush. He kept his head down. Kept running, kept dodging. Kept his trajectory random until, with a gasp of anxiety filled exhaustion, he launched himself over a low concrete wall around the back yard of the first house in Dry Mouth, smashing to the ground and rolling to a stop on his front.

Bullets slammed into the other side of the wall, throwing up jagged chips and billowing dust. Cody put his hand on his right bicep. The palm came away smeared with blood. The tear in his shirt was ragged, but the wound beneath was on the borderline of superficial. It was just another addition to the rest of the pain in his body.

Jack's jeans pocket began to vibrate.

Kelly's iPhone.

He'd completely forgotten that he still had it. They hadn't taken it away in Dry Mouth PD, and the damn thing was receiving a call! He pulled it from the pocket. The screen was cracked and scarred. The casing was bent, but the smartphone itself was still working.

"Yes?"

Cody got up and scrambled across the yard as he spoke. Bullets crashed into the house, but the further he was away from the church, the less accurate the shots were.

"Jack. Is that you?"

Jack vaulted a picket fence and ran around to the front of the property. Now the bullets couldn't find their target however accurate they were. He stopped to catch his breath, the iPhone still to his ear, bent double, clutching at the stitch in his side.

"Sara? Yes. It's me."

"Thank god. Jack, listen. I don't have much time."

"You and me both, sister."

"Are you still in Dry Mouth?"

"Yes."

"Get to Hacker. There are some things you need to tell him."

"I tried yesterday. He's not sure who he can trust, and he's not trusting a guy who walked out of the desert dressed like a hobo."

Jack began walking between the properties, looking for the access road he'd come in on originally from main street. The sky was lightening quickly. The dawn was no longer waiting timidly by the horizon. It was moving up the heavens in a blue wash of brightness.

"Try harder. Jack, there's so much to tell you. So, you have to listen and I'm gonna speak fast because I'm about to try to inveigle my ass into the White House under false pretenses."

"And you want to tell me that on an open unencrypted line?"

"Shush, Jack. I know what I'm doing. But like you, I don't know who I can trust. But I know I can trust you. In two hours, whatever Hacker does, the President, and whoever is inside the church is going to be dead."

"What...? How do you know...?"

"Doesn't matter. You have to get to Hacker and tell him, that at eight AM, there's going to be a bloodbath. It's all been a massive set up. Whatever happens. Whatever Elkins says or promises. *Everyone* in that church is going to die."

And then she told him how.

CHAPTER 34

When she'd finished, Sara clicked off the iPhone, and got out of the Evoque.

It had all sounded as crazy coming out of her mouth, and she wouldn't have blamed Jack if he thought she'd gone insane since their last meet. But Jack had taken it all in and said, "Okay. I'll try to get through to Hacker."

Sara had parked in a tow away zone on New York Avenue, just across the street from the Eisenhower Executive Office Building—she wouldn't need the Range Rover again—the cops could tow it away as much as they liked.

She had left Roger and Sullivan back in McClean gagged and handcuffed to an aluminum fence next to where she'd parked the Evoque.

She then dumped the flight cases in a storm drain on the way back across the river into the city.

She wouldn't be able to get a gun into the White House, or any other weapon for that matter, so she would have to use what she had. She'd found a silver-metal ball-point pen, a glass paperweight that fitted neatly inside Cortina's purse, and a toothbrush in the bathroom.

The toothbrush was the best weapon she had. They had been used for years as lethally effective shivs in prisons. All it took was two minutes of furious grating on rough brickwork, and the end of the handle would be sharp enough to puncture a lung or take out an eye.

The staff entrance to the West Wing was on Executive Avenue, and once the microchip in Cortina's pass had got her onto the street. Sara walked towards the canvas covered gazebo outside the West Wing, where pat downs and final checks were made by the security staff.

She had been to the White House many times, but never through this entrance, so it was a calculated risk that she'd get through without being recognized as not being the person on the picture card.

But it was a risk she had to take.

Sara beeped her card on the reader, was passed okay, and was given a bag search and a pat down. The security around the White House was much the same as it had always been, and she wondered if that again was another factor in how high the conspiracy went to the top. *Don't panic,* they'd have said, *don't show the American people we're scared and under threat—just keep it as business as usual.* And that attitude may have held Sara as much as it had been a PR victory for the conspirators.

The toothbrush's sharpened end had been wrapped in two tissues and hidden amongst the junk you'd find in any woman's purse. If she was called upon to explain the paperweight, she'd prepared a story about her niece who wanted her to put it on her desk while she worked.

But the bag got through without and she was inside.

The corridors in the West Wing were filled with streams of grave looking people. She scanned the faces of anyone who looked like they might recognize her so that she could change direction if she needed to and avoid them.

But she saw no one she'd dealt with before.

The usual hubbub of the building was absent. Even though everyone was there—usually getting in from 6am onwards in Sara's experience—the subdued nature in the place was all pervading. Even if the people at the top weren't feeling the threat, the workers, the press officers, the secretaries, the speech writers and the administrative staff surely were.

Sara looked at her watch.

10am Eastern, which meant it was 7am in Dry Mouth. One hour to work this from both ends. Sara at the White House, and Jack at the church. Both white buildings that used to represent hope, but now were stained with evil on the inside.

Sara only had a ghost of plan as she walked out of the West Wing now, into the opulence and stately majesty of the White House itself.

Sara took a lanyard from Cortina's bag and putting it around her neck, she attached the pass to it.

Passes were meant to be shown at all times. Sometimes in the EEOB and the West Wing, you could get away with it if you were known and had been through heavy security to gain entrance in the first place. But in the White House itself, she knew she would be stopped immediately if the pass wasn't around her neck.

She had to hope that her luck would hold.

It felt odd going into a building she had been in before as an official visitor—to advise the President's staff on the status of operations around the world—to now be here as interloper. She was used to going into situations which would be dangerous or difficult as a field agent, but not in such symbolically important places.

The Vice President's office was on the far side of the White House from where Sara had entered through the Palm Room, and it was not her final destination.

If Blake's information was correct, she'd need to travel through the Press Corps office, on through the briefing room, then take a left past the Cabinet Room to end up outside the President's Personal Secretary's office. After that she had only the vaguest ideas of what she would do.

She could see there were Marines in full dress uniform dotted throughout the building as she moved out of the Press Briefing room. There were Secret Service agents in evidence too. She hadn't been IDed yet. Maybe they didn't think she wouldn't be so stupid as try to get in here. Maybe they were all on edge and not at the top of their game, or maybe—and this was the sweetest hope of all—perhaps there was still a majority of people in the building who had not gone over.

As Sara came to the first obstacle she would have to negotiate to get into the Oval Office—the President's secretary—a hand fell on her shoulder. And Roger's voice said, "Well hello, Sara. Fancy meeting you here."

CHAPTER 35

"You look like someone put you in a blender," Kelly said.

"They pretty much did."

Jack had made it back to Kelly's over-the-shop apartment just before 7am, after dodging National Guardsmen and other instruments of authority the streets of Dray Mouth.

She'd opened the door when he'd knocked bleary eyed, let him inside and closed the door behind him.

"God, Jack! I'm sorry about what happened with Kellerman and Brant. Mike was too. We argued that they shouldn't have locked you up, but not no one was listening."

"I guessed Mike wasn't as happy with the whole thing when he put that shot over me, rather than *in* me."

"Kellerman said Mike was fired on the spot. Mike was already writing out his letter of resignation. If it wasn't for Tessa Pearce from the Town Council talking him out of it last night, he would have handed it in too."

Kelly came up for a hug, but Cody held up his hand. Kelly's

face fell. "No, it's not that," he told her. "I hurt and haven't stopped hurting for a while. As soon as I'm fixed you have all the hugs you want."

"Really?"

"Really. But first, I need to speak to Mike. Where is he?"

"The Police Department, I guess. I'm pretty sure he wouldn't have gone home last night."

"Then let's go."

The half of the town that hadn't been evacuated from the new exclusion zone, was waking up as they drove away from Kelly's auto shop. Hacker's Command Truck was across main street, with a ring of National Guard Tahoe's keeping people back.

Kelly swung her F-350 into the lot outside the library and they raced up the stairs to the Dry Mouth PD office.

Mike was taking phone calls and Tessa Pearce was working at a terminal. Sitting next to her was Brittany Franco. Mike looked up as he saw Cody and Kelly arriving. He said a quick goodbye into the receiver and came over. His face grim. "Man. I am sorry. Truly. Kellerman pulling rank... I shoulda told him where to stick his Police Department. In fact, after you got out, I almost did."

"Yeah," said Cody, "Kelly told me."

Tessa Pearce stopped typing and looked at the only remaining member of Dry Mouth PD. "I keep telling you, Mike. You don't have to worry about Kellerman anymore. Once Brittany has filed her story about him and Brant, I reckon the state legislature will have more than enough grounds for impeachment."

"Oh, yes indeed," Brittany agreed, typing onto a laptop. "We are gonna blow this state wide open with this."

"Once the President and the hostages are safe," Mike said quickly.

Brittany went a little red, but she nodded. "Of course, Mike, sorry."

Mike turned from the women planning Kellerman's demise, and looked contritely at Cody. "What can I do for you, man? I have no idea what you've been up to, Jack, but you look worse than a man who's sat on a saddle made of cactus."

"Thanks. I need you to get me into see Hacker. Can you do that?"

"I don't know that I can get you through the line, but I might be able to help you out in some other way." Mike picked up the nearest telephone from a desk. "I have his direct line. That any good to you?"

* * * * *

"I don't have time for this, Cody. You're persona non-grata."

"Hacker, I was contacted this morning by my contact in the CIA, Sara Durell. She's told me we're not to trust Elkins. It's all been a massive deception. They want to get the eyes of the United States on this church at eight AM. That's why they've been pushing that time so hard. The fourteen eighty-eight. The fourteen words and Heil Hitler it's the signal. The speech is just a side show. Sara told me everyone is going to die in there. It's part of the plan. They want maximum shock and chaos. We have to stop them, and we have to stop them *now*."

Hacker sighed. "I have no go order for an assault. I've been told to keep negotiating and to wear Elkins down. He can't keep up this forever. He'll start releasing hostages soon. All we gotta do is let him make his speech, and the profilers think he's going to stand down immediately after. He'll have done his thing."

Jack thumped the table. "No, Hacker. No. You've been told not to go in precisely *because* they need this moment to happen. We've all been played. Me, you all of us."

Hacker hesitated.

Jack could almost hear the cogs whirring in the Secret Service commander's head.

Come on. Come on.

Jack looked at the clock on the wall, 7.28 am. Thirty-two minutes to go.

Come on. *Come on.*

CHAPTER 36

"You think you're the only one who knows spy stuff like getting out of handcuffs?" Roger said. "You should have killed me when you had the chance. Looks like I headed you off at the pass just in time. You're not getting in there to interrupt the VP. You're coming with me, and you're going to die."

Sara looked around. There were Marines, there were secret service agents, and administrative works. Who could she trust? She didn't know.

But she wasn't going to let herself fall at the last hurdle.

"Don't touch me, you freak!" Sara shouted at Roger, turning heads in every direction. The nearest Marine sentry broke his stiff attention stance and looked momentarily confused. It was clear he wasn't used to people shouting in the White House, let alone outside the Oval Office.

Roger wasn't expecting it either. He looked at the hand that was on Sara's arm, then at the Marine, and back to Sara.

Yup, she thought, *you look guilty as hell.*

"This man just sexually assaulted me in the corridor! I've been assaulted! I've been assaulted! Please arrest him!"

Roger took a step back, reaching under his jacket. The Marine, an African American with the smoothest skin Sara had ever seen on his face may have been easy on the eye, but he was lighting with his reflexes. His service issue SIG-Sauer was already in his hand. "Do not reach for your weapon, sir. Put up your hands."

Roger's hands went up. The Marine covered him with the pistol, reached inside Roger's jacket, and pulled out his gun. "Can I get some assistance here?" the Marine called in the general direction of the Cabinet room. A second Marine and two Secret Service agents came running.

The President's secretary, a blousy, generally well-upholstered woman in her mid-fifties walked past Sara to see what all the fuss was about, and Sara floated back. Roger tried to tell the marines they were all making a big mistake. No one who'd arrived seemed to be ready to believe him, which gave Sara hope that not all of the White House had been overrun with 14/88ers.

The Secretary's Office was a domain of high efficiency and maximum tidiness, which had been compromised somewhat by a number of containers and cases stamped with network news logos. Sara skipped past them and opened the door to the Oval Office.

No point hesitating. If she was going to do this, she might as well do this right.

A room she'd seen a million times on TV, suddenly felt

so much larger than she ever imagined. Nearly thirty feet away, the Resolute Deck was being lit by engineers putting up lights. A director was chatting to his camera and sound guys. There were two monitors on wheels which so far were blank.

On the sofas equidistant between the door and the desk, Vice President Mulray was looking at a speech on a clipboard, scoring out lines and putting in addendums with furious concentration. She was sitting with a grey-haired man Sara knew to be the VP's chief of staff Bill Hadrian.

Mulray's eyes flicked up and back down to the paper. "At last, Cortina. Did one little conference in McClean really have to go on so long?"

Mulray had only noticed the suit, she hadn't bothered, in her moment of deep concentration on the speech, to check out the face of the woman who'd come in.

Sara had her moment. Just the one—and so she took it.

Sliding around the sofa she sat next to the Vice President and stuck the sharpened toothbrush in Mulray's side.

Sara smiled sweetly. "One failure to do what I say or to call for help and I'll gut you like a fish."

Mulray's eyes where wide but her mouth clamped shut. Bill Hadrian made to get up, and Sara flashed him a look which he caught like a slap. "I wouldn't if I were you, Hadrian. Sit down," she whispered, her face still set in a gloriously happy smile.

The director and his crew were a good fifteen feet away, discretely deep in conference or on the setup duty.

Sara whispered to Mulray, "Tell the crew to leave while *we* have a conference."

"Are you insane...?" Mulray responded quietly. "I'm not going to..."

Sara pushed the prison shiv further into Mulray's side, hoping to catch on a rib. Mulray grimaced and the point pierced the material of her blouse.

"Next one and I'll open you up."

Sara's eyes fixed on Mulray's.

The whirl of the last twenty-four hours twisting through her mind like a tornado about to cut across the landscape. The kidnap of the President. The beating of Debbie Langwith, the woman who had found out what was going on and tried to tell Sara. The terrorist bombing of a hospital to kill that same woman—then the attempts on Sara's life, and the savage beating of poor Agent Denis Barber. All to protect a conspiracy of epic proportions. A conspiracy that was culminating now in *this* room in Washington DC, and in a church in Dry Mouth, Arizona.

Two locations at either side of America, with the line connecting them like a bloody wound across the slashed throat of the republic.

Today there would see the death of one President, and the accession of the next. All played out center stage in a piece of political theatre arranged to coincide with a meaningful date for racists and bigots everywhere.

Racists and bigots who had now been armed to the teeth, who would flock and rally around a Populist President like Mulray. One who would rule over a land burning with fear-induced hatred and the worship of an ideology putting racial supremacy and purity at the heart of it—rather the indomitability of the human spirit.

Sara dug the shiv deeper into the Mulray's side. "I said tell them to leave. Now. We're going to rewrite your speech."

CHAPTER 37

The red, blue and gold Arizona Department of Corrections Bell 206 Jet Ranger landed fifty feet from *Marine One*.

Even before the rotors begun to slow down, the side door opened, and Honeychild Elkins bounded across the grass towards the steps of the church, whooping and calling to her father, hair flying in the gale.

She ran past a single news channel camera that had been set up on Jud's orders, with a large directional microphone pointed at the door of the church. The TV crew who had finished setting up the equipment, were running away from the church in their bulky tactical vests.

Honeychild paused to wave at them as they went.

Bo pulled the door open, and Honeychild ran inside.

She pounded down the aisle and threw herself around Jud, wrapping arms and legs around her father and, looking over his shoulder to flip the bird at President Harwood.

The sound of the helicopter that had delivered her clattered through the church as it took off again. A gust of rotor induced wind blew in via the window Bo had poured bullets through at the running man just over an hour before.

"Daddy! Daddy! You done sprung me!"

"I certainly did, Honeychild. How they been treating my prettiest and smartiest?"

"Bleurgh! Prison food sucks, the place is full of lesbians and illegals and black-trash!"

Honeychild jumped down and skipped to hug her mother and brother simultaneously. She looked about, seemingly uninterested in the hostages, or the priest, Pickles, Blint or the SWAT team.

"Where's Tod, Daddy? Tell me he's ok?!"

Jud smiled, holding up an encrypted smartphone of his own. "Of course, he is. He'll be here real soon."

Jud turned to Pickles and Harwood. "I reckon we should get ready for your speech, Mister President. What do you say?"

"I say you're a worm, Elkins, and you can make your own damn speech."

Jud closed his eyes. "Oh, Mister President, I wish you hadyna said that."

Jud raised his gun and shot Reverend Just through the forehead where he was sitting. The old priest fell across David Cody, a fountain of blood slopping out of the wound, running across the floor and over David's shoes.

"You hateful bastard!" David screamed, pushing Reverend Just's body to the boards and getting up with a roar.

Bo stepped in and felled the curate with one punch to the gut, then pressed his boot hard down on David's head, pinning him to the floor. "Don't you curse at my daddy, you no good piece of shit."

"Enough of this!" Pickles shouted, coming down off the altar. "You've had your fun, and you've got your daughter. Now you have work to do, Elkins. Get ready!"

Pickles' face was sheened with sweat. His arms were trembling, and Jud had noticed several times in the last few hours the Secret Service agent has been watching his timepiece more than he'd been watching the President.

"We have time, Pickles. Stop fussing."

Jud leaned over and pulled the President to his feet. "You want to pick the next one to die if you don't do as you're told? We certainly have more bullets than hostages."

Harwood shook his head. "I'll read your statement. I'll do it."

"Good boy," Jud said putting a dog's choke chain around the President's neck. "Let's go."

But as they walked by Bo, Jud whispered in his ear. "Keep your eye on Pickles. Something ain't right."

Bo nodded. Jud and Sandra walked with the President to the vestibule.

Honeychild began to dance.

* * * * *

The noise was hellish this close to the engine, and in the fourteen cubic feet of baggage bay, even though it had been hastily stripped to the bare minimum of fittings, was still a cramped and inhospitable space.

The Jet Ranger taking off again was the signal for Cody to release the catch on the inside of the door, and to open it a tiny crack. The plan was for the Jet Ranger to take off as soon as Honeychild was inside the church, and for Cody to ready himself.

He would only get *one* chance at this.

Using the helicopter to get close to the church without being spotted from the inside, causing Jud to start killing the President and the hostages, was calculated madness. But it had to be tried. The scheme was hastily agreed by Hacker, once Cody had explained everything and he'd run to the command truck on main street.

Hacker had spoken to Cody away from anyone in his team who might have passed on information to Jud or the others. "This is a whole other level of crazy." The Secret Service commander had said.

"I can do it. Just get me there," Cody replied, trying not to wince too much as his aching body sang with pain.

"Okay," Hacker had said, responding to the earnestness and confidence in Cody's tone.

Hacker ordered the Jet Ranger to land first in Dry Mouth on the pretense of refueling, so Cody could be smuggled on board by Mike and Kelly into the baggage bay. It had to be done without alerting Honeychild who was cuffed in the passenger seat to a corrections officer. As she was too busy singing to herself and giggling, it hadn't been as difficult as they imagined.

The rest would be down to Jack.

The helicopter lifted quickly and began to turn. The cracked open baggage bay door showed a dizzying spiral of grass, then church, then spire above the bell tower. One chance. No rehearsal, and if he missed, no possibility to try again.

Three.

Two.

One.

It was a fifteen-foot drop to the spire, made all the more dicey by the downdraft from the helicopter. But it was a double-edged sword. The sound of the clashing rotor blades should cover Cody hitting the spire and grappling on.

Cody leapt through the air. The spire came up fast and hard. And Cody's already injured chest felt like it was going to explode as he smashed into it.

Jack grabbled for a handhold and kicked about for purchase for his toes as he, still buffeted by the helicopter, began his struggle against gravity.

Bumping down the fifteen feet of black tiles beneath the high metal cross, Cody dug his heels in and hugged the spire, even pressing down with his chin to throw more friction onto his descent. He came to a stop, just above the raked lip above the bell tower. His knees were barked and his elbows raw.

But he'd done it.

Well, at least the first part of his plan.

He was clinging to the west aspect of the bell tower, and the steep roof over the main body of the church was behind him. Only someone with a view of the back or side of the church would be able to spot him.

But as he'd seen the muzzle flashes of the sniper rifle from inside the community church's small bell tower when he'd run past in the last dark of the night, he knew that if the sniper was still there, he wouldn't been able to see him jumping, hear him land, or see him now.

Of course, if the sniper had moved to a vantage point outside the church, then Jack Cody was a dead man.

No shot came.

The sniper was still in the bell tower.

Jack unhooked the paracord from his belt and sent the weighted end curling around the bell tower, catching it between his quick fingers as it snaked around. Tying the lines together then attaching it to his harness, Cody pulled the cord tight and leapt off into space again.

Swinging though the windowless back section of the bell tower, he came feet first and then face to face with Tod Elkins.

The boy was trying to bring his .308 Winchester sniper rifle to bear as Cody's feet connected with his belly and he was kicked backwards. The church bell was made of a black iron casting, static and rung by an electronic clapper from the church below. As Tod crashed into it, it hardly made a sound, and he hit it hard.

The Winchester tumbled from Tod's grip, falling to the floorboards. Cody punched the boy in the gut and kicked his knee so that it snapped straight and the boy howled.

Jack chopped the boy's Adam's apple and the howl was cut off into a sick gurgle. Tod put one hand on his throat and another on his hip, pulling a Bowie knife from his belt.

Trying to speak but now having no voice, Tod stabbed at Cody with the knife.

Jack caught the boy's wrist, snapped the arm at the elbow with a crunching blow with his forearm, curled a length of paracord around Tod's neck and used it to drag him towards the opening he'd made and threw him through.

Tod's neck snapped as his body juddered to a halt.

Jack tied the free end of the cord around the top of the ladder leading into the church to secure the body and started his descent.

CHAPTER 38

Jud pushed the President to his knees and Bo opened the doors to the world. The helicopter was almost away in the distance now. The hour struck eight o'clock and the festivities were about to begin.

Jud put the speech written by Sandra into the President's hands and put the gun to the back of his head. "Read it."

Harwood's shoulders sagged. His head dropped, holding the paper in trembling fingers, but he began to read.

"My fellow Americans. I today relinquish the office of President. I have come to realize that white collar criminals are responsible for this great country of ours going down the tubes. The billionaires have been sitting in Congress and in the White House and the Pentagon and have not only filched the earnings and savings of everyday honest hardworking people, but they've tossed those very taxpayers to the wolves when they found they could fatten their purses even more by sending jobs to cheap labor in Third World countries. Assembled in Washington are the vessels of evil who have conspired to use elected office to drive into the ground the very people who have elected them. And I have been complicit in that. I am as guilty as all of them. And if Jud Elkins and the Pledge Holder's demands are not met, then I deserve to die here and now. It is only right that I should meet my atonement in the house of the Lord, and through Judd Elkins the instrument of His wrath."

Jud snorted at the notion but didn't say anything. All good theatre requires a script. Harwood hesitated again, and so Jud pushed the gun harder into the back of his head. "Carry on, Mister Ex-President."

Harwood's voice cracked, but he continued. "History does not long entrust the care of freedom to the weak or the timid. The Pledge Holders and the fourteen eighty-eight movement are ready to assume control—to give the White Race back the respect it has lost to the fools, the immigrants and the snow-flakes. Today is the dawning of the new age. Today America shall rise and…"

* * * * *

The bell tower door to the right of the vestibule was kicked open and Cody came out firing two Glocks, one in each hand.

Bo went down with a bullet to the chest, kicking up a spray of blood.

Jud was already propelling himself backward, pulling the President on the choke chain, keeping Harwood between himself and Cody so that he didn't have a clear shot.

The SWAT team and the Secret Service agents opened fire, but Cody was rolling into the church, ducking behind the pews, and letting the heavy wood take all the punishment.

Bullets chewed across floor as Blint started shooting low, beneath the pews. The clatter of bullets from the SWAT team ended almost simultaneously as they emptied their magazines at once.

"Schoolboy error, guys," said Cody.

He stuck his head up and fired four rounds. The SWAT team went down as four headshots found marks in three skulls. Scrambling over the floor, Cody made it to McDaniel's coffin which was still on the wheeled gurney. Pushing the whole assembly along and using it for cover. He triggered a burst over the top, putting a bullet in Blint.

Pickles was using Pavlina Harwood for cover and was looking at his dying comrade, fifteen feet away.

Pickles shouted to Blint, "Throw it to me! Throw it to me!"

Jud, choking the chain around Harwood's neck and still using him as a human shield, screamed, "Stop firing or I'll blow this place up. All of us."

Henri stood up. "No! Don't! Please! Not me! Please!"

Jack let off another two shots as Sandra tried to run across the church to hide with her husband behind the President.

She went down as one bullet slammed into her pelvis, and the other into the side of her ear sending her spinning into a lectern.

"Throw it! Blint! For god's sake don't just lay there dying.

Throw it here!" Pickles was still screaming. Blint had stopped moving.

Jud looked at the bodies of his wife, and then Bo in the vestibule. His face red and tear stained. The choke chain was so tight around the President's throat, Harwood was turning blue. Pretty soon Jud was going to have to hold him up himself.

Jack watched as Jud reached into his pocket and brought out the detonator.

Henri fell to his knees pulling his shirt wide, wildly displaying the plastic explosives and the wires.

"Please! No!"

"Honeychild, come here," Jud instructed his daughter, who was sprawled on the floor with her arms covering her head.

Pickles fired two shots at Cody behind the coffin, but they slammed ineffectually into the wood and brass as he ducked.

Honeychild got up and moved towards Jud. Pickles had given up trying to get Blint to do what he asked, so he began to drag Pavlina towards his dead or dying comrade instead.

"I'm gonna detonate! I'm gonna blow this sucker!" Jud held onto the President and wrapped the arm with the detonator around Honeychild's shoulders. He kissed the top of her head and said. "I'm sorry."

The hostages, still zip-locked together, screamed and cowered beneath each other, trying to push themselves through the walls.

As Jud thumbed the detonator, David Cody came out of the shadows at the back of the church where he'd been hiding from the gunfire and threw himself across Henri. He took the Frenchman down trying to smother the explosion with his own body.

Time stood still.

Then…

Nothing happened.

Jack changed both magazines and stuck his head up from behind the coffin.

"You've been taken for a sucker, Jud." He called. "They've had you for a patsy. The plastic explosives you put on Henri Charon, given to you by fourteen eighty-eight were never meant to explode. They didn't think you had the guts to do it anyway, but they really didn't want you fouling up by blowing up the President early or by accident."

Jud kept pressing the detonator.

Jack came out from behind McDaniel's coffin and pointed his guns at Pickles who was still behind Pavlina.

Pickles who was halfway to Blint now, tried to fire at Cody, but his gun was empty.

Jack kept walking.

Jud didn't have a free hand to reach for a gun, what with hiding behind the President and pressing the useless detonator.

"The actual bomb has been outside the whole time. Blint and Pickles loaded a suitcase device onto Marine One when they took off to come here today with the President. You were just a side show, Jud. Used to rally the faithful militia in the country. The front. You thought you were going to get out of here. You believed them when they told you that you would."

Pickles kept dragging Pavlina. He was five feet from Blint now.

"That's why you had Honeychild brought here. They were right about you, Jud. You're a self-serving idiot who believes everything he's told. Once you'd got the President to deliver the speech, the bomb on Marine One would have been detonated. Destroying the church and everyone in it. It would be the signal to avenge the Martyrs. And it almost worked."

Pickles reached Blint's body and put a free hand into the dead man's jacket. He withdrew a small silver box and held it up.

"No, it worked. You're dead, and the revolution begins now!"

The explosion sent a shockwave across the desert that reverberated through the church. But it didn't damage it.

Pickles face was a filled with confusion. "But..."

Jack took the silver box from Pickles fingers and threw it across the room.

"Mike Wilson travelled with me here. While Honeychild was taking all your attention, he snuck into *Marine One*, removed the bomb and transferred it to the other helicopter. They dropped it three miles away. Your revolution just blew up its first cactus."

Jud screamed, threw down his detonator and pulled the pistol from his belt. Harwood, almost choked to death now, collapsed to the floor, pulling at the chain around his throat.

Jud shot Pickles. Cody shot Jud.

CHAPTER 39

"My fellow Americans, I speak to you today from the Oval Office to confess to my crimes of treason. To admit to you all that I, with others, planned and executed a conspiracy to assassinate President Harwood, and have me take over in his place. We wanted to start a civil war in this country that would change it forever, and would certainly have resulted in the deaths of thousands, maybe hundreds of thousands of people. Myself and others incited Jud Elkins and his Pledge Holders to violence. We helped him hide from justice, we gave him succor and we gave him assistance. We hoped that his network of Citizen Militias, who we have armed and also encouraged, would rise up and destroy the institutions that you all hold dear. We hoped to usher in an administration that would have taken away all the rights and freedoms guaranteed to you by the Constitution of the United States. But our plan has failed. I am here now explaining to you that President Harwood will soon be on his way back to Washington and will re-assume control. I also have to tell you that agents still loyal to the government and their agencies are waiting here in the Oval Office for me to finish this speech. I am to be arrested and fully expect to be charged with treason at a later date. This will be my last address from this office as your Vice President. I hope that one day, you all may find it in your minds to understand me, if not in your hearts to forgive me. Goodbye, and God Bless America."

EPILOGUE

"Don't call me that!"

"But it's true. You're the woman who saved the United States with a toothbrush."

"Jack, you're not funny."

"I so am, and now I shall call you a kicking-assiest Dentist in the history of the CIA."

They walked arm in arm through the warm Boston afternoon. October was a step away, but the trees were still green, the air sweet and the lightly cloud-scudded sky an endless blue.

"What will you do?"

"I still haven't decided."

"What did David say?"

"He invited me to stay with him. He wants to pull the distance between us tighter. He might want me to help out at the church."

"You? A *church*?"

"I shot it up quite a bit. He's gonna need some help fixing it up. I owe him at least that."

"I guess."

"What about you?"

"Me? I don't know. Everything seems very up in the air. I'll have to testify before congress, and I'll get caught up in the trials, I'm sure. But after that—I don't know what my place will be. There are a lot of Militia out there with a ton of free weaponry. Someone's got to clean that mess up. There will be a fourteen eighty-eight every year. The threat will not go away."

They stopped walking at their destination and stood in silence for a moment.

"I don't know what to say," Sara said.

"I don't think you need to say anything."

And so they didn't.

After three minutes, where all they could hear were the rustling trees, and the distant roar of Boston traffic, Sara turned and hugged Cody. He hugged her back. Tight.

"I guess you're off then?" Sara said.

"The earth never stops moving beneath my feet."

"Don't walk too far."

"If I do, I'll only come all the way around again."

"Good."

Cody kissed her on the end of the nose.

"Coming?"

Sara shook her head. "I'll stay a little while longer. You go."

"Okay, Woman who Saved America with a Toothbrush,

see you around."

Sara smiled. "Count on it."

Jack walked back along the path, towards the F-350 and Kelly who was waiting there.

Sara turned and read again the legend carved into the stone.

"Here lies a true American Hero. He gave up his life so others could live in Freedom."

Sara reached into her purse and pulled out a china coffee cup. She kissed it gently and put it down on the headstone of Denis Barber.

IF YOU LIKED "CODY'S WAR" YOU MIGHT LIKE: "RETRIBUTION: A TEAM REAPER THRILLER"

EVERYTHING COMES AT A COST...

After he is betrayed and shoots the two most powerful men in the Irish Mob, John "Reaper" Kane is forced into hiding. He thinks Retribution, Arizona, is the perfect hiding place, but he is wrong. Underneath the old, crusty surface of the dying town, hides the Montoya Cartel, for they use it as a funnel to ship their drugs across the border.

Trying to lay low in a town gripped with lawlessness is impossible for the ex-recon marine, especially after the local sheriff is brutally murdered by the Montoya Cartel's sicario, leaving an old friend, Deputy Sheriff Cara Billings, the only person standing between them and the town.

Things go from bad to worse when Kane is arrested by Cleaver, the deputy in the cartel's pocket, for shooting a local gang member.

Enter DEA Agent Luis Ferrero who has expressed to his bosses for a long time the need for a task force to fight the cartels on their own ground. He's about to get his wish, and to head up his team, he wants the Reaper.

A thrill ride that doesn't let you go – Retribution is the first novel in the action-packed Reaper Series.

ABOUT THE AUTHOR

Stephen Mertz is an American fiction author who is best known for his mainstream thrillers and novels of suspense. His work covers a wide variety of styles from paranormal dark suspense (Night Wind and Devil Creek) to historical speculative thrillers (Blood Red Sun) and hardboiled noir (Fade to Tomorrow). Mertz is also a popular lecturer on the craft of writing and has appeared as a guest speaker before writer's groups and at universities.

Steve's writing output increased dramatically when he emerged as one of the country's most in-demand writers of adventure paperback novels, averaging four books per year for ten years. His work on Don Pendleton's Mack Bolan series is regarded by fans as some of the best in that series. He also created the Mark Stone: MIA Hunter and Cody's Army series, written under the pseudonyms Jack Buchanan and Jim Case respectively.

Stephen Mertz lives in the American Southwest, and he is always at work on a new book.

Find Stephen online: www.stephenmertz.com